GOOD NEWS/
BAD NEWS

GOOD NEWS/ BAD NEWS

by
Philip M. Fragasso

Addison-Wesley

Copyright © 1980 by Philip M. Fragasso
All Rights Reserved
Addison-Wesley Publishing Company, Inc.
Reading, Massachusetts 01867
Printed in the United States of America

ABCDEFGHIJK-DO-89876543210

Library of Congress Cataloging in Publication Data

Fragasso, Philip M
    Good news/bad news.

    SUMMARY: Rivalry between two highschool newspapers causes
problems between Leonard and Jessie, twins on the staff of one, and
between Leonard and his girlfriend Rebecca, who is on the staff of the
other.
    [1. Journalism — Fiction.   2.   Twins — Fiction.
3.   School stories]   I.   Title.

PZ7.F843Go   [Fic]   80-15582
                ISBN 0-201-03197-3

For Grandma Lillie

CHAPTER

My SISTER Jessie should be the one telling this story. She's by far the best writer in the family, and the story is mostly about her. But she's been pretty busy lately with the school newspaper and going out with Rick, so she says she doesn't have the time. That's probably the truth, but I think part of it is that she's still bothered by the whole thing and would rather forget that it ever happened. So I guess it's up to me.

Jessie and I are twins. I almost wrote "identical twins," but that really wouldn't be possible since we're brother and sister. Anyway, I guess we're as identical as fraternal twins can possibly be. At least that's what everybody says. Personally I can't see all that much of a resemblance. I mean aside from the obvious biological differences that any bright three-year-old could recognize, there are quite a few distinguishing characteristics. For one thing I'm smarter — even if she is a better writer. For another thing her hair is a little darker brown than mine, and I'm a good inch or two taller. Jessie also has a lot more freckles than I do, but most of them are on her shoulders — which means that they only show when she's wearing a halter top, which means that they only show when Dad isn't around. Dad's a little conservative when it comes to Jessie. He's not so bad with me.

I've got to give Mom and Dad credit, though, because aside from a few problem areas — like halters, *Playboy* magazine, curfews, and a couple of other things that I don't even want to remind them about — they're pretty decent people. The best thing about them is that they didn't stick us with a set of those stupid matching names that a lot of parents like to give twins. You've probably heard about some of them: Twin brothers and sisters named Jack and Jill, or Romeo and Juliet, or something equally insane. At least our parents had the common sense to name us Leonard (everybody calls me Lenny) and Jessica (as you've undoubtedly already guessed, everybody calls her Jessie). So we've really got nothing to complain about in that area.

By the way, we also have a younger brother, Andrew, who's just turned eight and shows every sign of being the much-sought-after missing link between man and monkey. But he's a whole other story. (If I were going to write about Andrew's life I'd probably start off with "My brother Andrew is a complete and total pain in the butt," and then take it from there.)

As I said, this story is mainly about Jessie, so I'll start off by telling you something about her. She's pretty enough that even I notice how pretty she is. Since I'm her brother you can imagine what the other guys think. She's probably the third or fourth best looking girl in the school — depending on whether or not you're counting Barbara Larson, who was suspended for showing up drunk at the homecoming dance and then throwing up all over Mr. Samuels, the assistant principal.

Jessie has long, dark-dark brown hair that hangs halfway down her back. She usually parts it in the middle, and rather than using a bobby pin to keep it out of the way, she's constantly pushing it back away from her eyes. I'm sure she thinks it's sexy, and from the comments I hear, she's right.

"That's some sister you've got, Lenny. Can you set me up with her?"

Or:

"I'd give my right arm for an hour alone with her."

Or:

"What does she look like in her nightgown?"

Or:

— Well, some of the guys can get pretty raunchy so I think I'll stop it there.

Jessie takes most of it in stride. Since she's always been prettier than other girls, it probably seems like the most natural thing in the world, and she doesn't let it affect her.

It's the same with her writing. She's a natural. She can take the dullest subject and make it interesting. Personally, I can't stand to write term papers, but I make sure that I read every single one that Jessie writes because they're always so good. Last semester she wrote a paper on mushrooms for Old Man Johnston's science class. Now in this whole wide world there are very few things uglier or more boring than mushrooms, but I swear to you that by the time Jessie was done describing them I practically wanted to *be* a mushroom, they sounded so good. She's really got a talent.

Mr. Polansky thought so, too, because he appointed her editor-in-chief of the student newspaper. That's a nice feather in anybody's cap, but what made it even better was that Jessie was the first junior to be given the top job. Before that the position had been given only to seniors. So as I say, it was quite an honor. And it was so obvious that Jessie had the best qualifications for the job that only one person complained about it.

3

As everyone expected, Mr. Personality himself, Steve Braverman, was not at all pleased with the decision. After all, as he protested to anyone who would listen, he *was* a senior and he *did* have three years' experience with the paper. And if I'm going to be at all truthful, I have to say that he's also a good writer. But that's the only nice thing you can say about him. Mostly he's sneaky and lazy.

Steve is the kind of guy who does only what he likes and avoids everything else like the plague. He glories in seeing his name in print, and he'll put in just enough work to see it gets there — not a single ounce more. Since he liked to cover football games and student plays, he usually did a good job of reporting them. Occasionally, when the mood struck him, he would even write an intelligent editorial on why students should be allowed to smoke in designated areas of the schoolyard or on how the girls' field hockey team could use some moral support. But that was about as far as he would go. When it came to the nitty gritty work of putting the newspaper together, Steve was always off somewhere, leaving the dirty work of typing and paste-up to "the kids" (the endearing term he used to refer to anyone more than six months younger than himself). Steve Braverman is a pompous jerk, and luckily Mr. Polansky had the sense to see that.

So Jessie started off her junior year as editor-in-chief of the *Tarmac*. And she had already made one enemy.

CHAPTER 2

JESSIE and I attend Fairfield High School, which is located just north of the center of town. It's a long, modern-looking, brick building that could probably pass for a bowling alley if you didn't look too closely. There's been a lot of talk lately about adding a new wing to the building, but I think they're probably waiting for somebody rich to die and leave the school a bundle of money. If that happens they'll probably have to rename the place So-and-So Memorial High School, but that can be done easily enough.

Well, maybe it wouldn't be so easy. All of the sports teams at Fairfield are called the "Flyers," and I have to admit that I really like the sound of the "Fairfield Flyers." It has a nice ring to it. If some old guy named Raginowitz died and left the school a lot of money, there could be some problems. I mean the "Raginowitz Flyers" just doesn't make it in my book. But I imagine that something could be worked out.

The Fairfield High newspaper is called the *Tarmac*. Now the first time I heard that it sounded pretty stupid, but it's quite appropriate once you learn what it means. A tarmac is the paved area surrounding an airplane hangar.

5

Since everything else at Fairfield refers to Flyers, it makes a lot of sense to have a newspaper named after a place where flyers can come home for a little rest and relaxation. I don't know who thought of the name, but I'd love to shake his hand. It was a stroke of genius.

Jessie was appointed editor at the year's first meeting of the *Tarmac*. It was a beautiful September day with a refreshing breeze that was filled with the scents of freshly picked apples and newly-mowed grass. Nobody, not even the teachers, wanted to be in school that day, but those of us who had any involvement at all with the *Tarmac* really struck out: We had to stay around *after* school. The meeting started at 3:30.

Mr. Polansky is a wonderful, gray-haired man who's getting close to retirement age. A few years ago he suffered a minor heart attack that kept him out of school for about two months, and some people thought he was going to call it quits then. But he came back that year, and he came back the year after, and he's still around now. Most of the time he looks like he could go on forever. My father remembers him as a teacher back when he was a boy, and even then he was the faculty advisor to the *Tarmac*. In his social studies class, Mr. Polansky has a reputation for being a hard marker, but no one ever complains that he's been unfair. He simply expects a lot from his students. And he expects even more from the staff of the *Tarmac*.

The first part of the meeting was a basic introduction to what the *Tarmac* was, what types of jobs were involved, who was eligible, and that kind of information. Most of us had heard it before, but Mr. Polansky was speaking mainly for the benefit of the five or six scared freshmen who were huddled together in the far corner of the room.

My attention span is not what it used to be, and since

I'm not very involved with the paper (mostly I just help out with proofreading and layout), my mind started to drift. I started out daydreaming about the upcoming baseball playoffs, but then I switched to whether or not I had any chance of dating the blond transfer student who sat in front of me in math. Her name is Rebecca, and rumor has it that she used to go out with the hotshot star quarterback at Roosevelt High School. Evidently she had been a cheerleader at Roosevelt, so when I heard that she was going to try out for the Fairfield cheerleading squad, I made sure that I'd be around to watch it. It was well worth the effort. She put all the other girls to shame, and if I'd known her only a little bit better, I would have fallen in love right then and there. She smiled at me when she finished her audition and I said hello. Maybe my chances with her were better than I had anticipated. Maybe I could study day and night and become a regular Einstein in math, and maybe then I could help her with her homework, and maybe . . .

". . . So except for Jessica and Steven, the rest of you may go. We'll have another meeting on Tuesday."

The frantic shuffling of tables and chairs as everybody hurried out the door snapped me to attention. I smiled at Mr. Polansky and waved a quick goodbye to Jessie. I probably also would have said goodbye to Steve, but he was staring straight ahead at the blackboard like some kind of zombie and wouldn't have noticed anyway. That night Jessie filled me in on what took place.

Mr. Polansky began by telling them how wonderful they both were. He explained that every year at this time he had to decide on a new editor.

"Believe me," he said, "it gets harder every year. Back in the old days when I was just starting out here at Fairfield, we were lucky to find two or three students who could even write an intelligent sentence. Nowadays most of you are good enough that you can realistically contemplate professional careers in journalism."

Mr. Polansky paused for a few moments and nervously cleared his throat. Jessie noticed that his face was flushed and he kept fidgeting with his tie.

"Needless to say, both of you are qualified for the job. However, it is not a position that can be shared. Over the summer I've given the matter a great deal of thought, and I feel that I must do what I believe is right. Therefore, I have decided to ask Jessica to serve as editor-in-chief of the *Tarmac*."

Jessie was thrilled beyond belief. She had dreamed about this all summer but never really expected it to come true. Now she felt like jumping up and down and shouting for joy. Then she looked over at Steve.

As soon as Mr. Polansky finished his announcement, Steve slumped down in his chair and closed his eyes. His face and ears were flushed a bright crimson, and Jessie could see his Adam's apple bobbing up and down his throat. His hands were clenched tightly around the edge of the desk. For a moment it looked like he was about to scream.

Jessie felt a little frightened and looked toward Mr. Polansky for comfort. He smiled but his face was strained, which only served to increase her anxiety.

"It's only natural," said Mr. Polansky, "that this is a big disappointment to you, Steven, but I would like to ask you to stay on with the paper as assistant editor. We've worked together for the past three years and your experience would be a tremendous asset to Jessica and the rest of the staff."

Mr. Polansky waited for a reply but received no indication that Steve had even heard the offer. He motioned for

Jessie to leave the room and whispered a reminder about the Tuesday meeting. As she closed the door, Jessie heard a loud slam as Steve banged his fist against the top of the desk, knocking a pile of books to the floor.

"You can't do this to me!" he shouted. "You've got no right to do this!" His voice broke into a high-pitched whine and he sounded like he was on the verge of tears.

Jessie clutched her pocketbook to her chest and ran down the hallway, not wanting to see or hear anything more. She had been editor of the paper for less than five minutes and already the glamour and prestige of the job were lost to her. All she could see was Steve's hurt and anger and somehow she felt responsible.

When she walked out of the school building that day, she had little doubt that it was going to be a long, troublesome year. She only hoped it would be worth it.

CHAPTER 3

I SOMETIMES think that the United States Post Office could learn a lot just by hanging around Fairfield for a couple of days. News travels so fast around here that you hardly have time to react to one rumor before another one comes along to expand or deny the first one. All in all it makes for interesting lunchtime conversation, but when you're stuck in the middle of it, it provides nothing but grief.

By the next morning, word of Jessie's appointment had reached three-fourths of the school, and it seemed like all of them wanted to express their personal congratulations and best wishes. It was a complete mob scene around Jessie's locker, so I stood close by in case she needed any help. She did.

Just before the 9:00 bell when everyone was due in homeroom, Steve showed up with a protective squad of three Neanderthal types, who looked like they would have difficulty spelling their own names. I moved so that I was standing right beside Jessie. She looked cool and calm, but I could see that she was nervous.

"So tell me," said Steve mockingly, "how did the big-shot editor sleep last night? Did you dream about winning the Pulitzer Prize? I mean today it's the *Tarmac*, maybe tomorrow it'll be *The New York Times*." Steve laughed and his gorilla henchmen followed his example. "But then again," he continued, "you can never tell what's gonna happen tomorrow."

Jessie kept her eyes fastened to Steve's and looked every bit his equal in determination. She gathered together a notebook and two textbooks from her locker and closed the metal door. She snapped shut the combination lock and walked right up to Steve, so that their faces were no more than a couple of inches apart.

"You know what I like about you, Steve?" she asked. Her voice was strong and even-tempered. Steve shook his head and decorated his face with what he probably thought was an evil-looking smirk.

Jessie paused for effect before completing her statement. Then she spoke slowly and carefully, stretching each syllable to its utmost.

"Absolutely nothing," she said.

Steve looked like he had just been hit in the stomach with a Nolan Ryan fastball. He opened his mouth to reply but nothing came out.

Jessie placed her hand around my arm and together we walked down the hall to homeroom.

We had won the battle, but the war had only just begun.

CHAPTER 4

T HE regularly scheduled Tuesday meeting of the *Tarmac* went off without a hitch. Jessie welcomed her staff and offered a few opening remarks.

"I'm not going to stand here in front of you and act like there's nothing at all unusual going on. As all of you know, my selection as editor has created a few problems, but they're the kind of problems that nobody but myself really needs to worry about. Mr. Polansky and I have discussed the situation and we're both anxious to get on with the business of putting this newspaper together. As originally announced, our first deadline for editorial copy will be one week from today."

Since Steve had made it very clear that he no longer wanted to remain on the staff, it was Mr. Polansky's responsibility to appoint a new assistant editor. With a minimum of fuss he selected Rick Acheson, a tall, lanky senior who was a varsity wrestler and co-captain of the debating team. I liked him well enough, but Jessie was all goofy-eyed about him.

"Don't you think he's just gorgeous?" she would ask.

"Not particularly," I would reply. "Actually, I think he's kind of skinny."

"Skinny! He's one solid hunk of muscle. And anyway he's better off being skinny than chubby, like that Rebecca you're so crazy about."

"Chubby! You've got to be kidding me. The only places Rebecca is chubby is where girls are supposed to be chubby. You're just jealous."

"And you're just a jerk."

That was the statement that always ended our arguments. Sometimes Jessie said it and sometimes I said it; but it was a clear signal that the teasing had gone on long enough. It was a line over which we seldom stepped.

So with the copy deadline rapidly approaching, we both began working on our assignments. Jessie was writing an editorial on the pros and cons of modular scheduling, a system that the school administration had been talking about for the last two or three years. I was supposed to cover the football team and come up with a set of scientifically-designed predictions for the upcoming season. Normally, I couldn't care less about that kind of thing, but since Rebecca was one of the cheerleaders, I was anxious to make a good impression. I attended every practice and filled up half a spiral notebook with quotes and personal comments from the coach, players, and of course, the cheerleaders. I spent a good day and a half writing the article, and I was very pleased with the result, which is unusual for me.

A couple of days after the copy deadline, Jessie and Rick met at our house to look over the articles that had been submitted. Since this was going to be the first edition of the *Tarmac* with them at the controls, they wanted it to be a good one. I stayed around for a while trying to be helpful, but it was obvious that they wanted to be alone. I mean when a guy and girl are practically sitting on top of each other on a couch that is large enough to hold as many as five people, you've got to figure that they'd like a little privacy.

I went downstairs to the family room and turned on the television. Since Mom and Dad were out with their bowling league, I went to the refrigerator and popped open a can of beer. I'm really not much of a drinker, especially compared to some of the kids at school, but an occasional beer helps me relax. It's soothing. In fact, this one was so soothing that I fell asleep halfway through the only *Star Trek* episode that I had seen less than three times. Jessie came down to get me at about 10:30.

"Wake up, Lenny. Mom and Dad are going to be home soon."

I opened my eyes very, v-e-r-y slowly. I yawned two or three times and rolled my eyes around their sockets trying to remember who I was, where I was, and what I was supposed to be doing. Suddenly, in a flash, it all came back to me. I stretched my arms and legs and stood up from the couch.

"So," I asked, mumbling my words with another yawn, "how did it go with you and lover boy? Get a lot of work done?"

I gave a little laugh and puckered my mouth in an exaggerated kiss. Jessie didn't even smile so I figured something was bothering her.

"Rick is sure that Steve is going to try and cause some problems for us," she said. "He's seen Steve talking to some of his idiotic friends, and he's sure they're planning something. Only he doesn't know what."

"Now let me guess, my sweet, dearly beloved sister," I said. "It's up to *me* to find out the mysterious 'what,' isn't it? Correct me if I'm wrong and reward me lavishly if I'm right, but that is my distinct impression."

"Yes, Mr. Know-it-all, you're right once again. But your only reward will be my eternal love and sisterly devotion. So see what you can do, you big jerk."

It's probably hard for you to believe, but Jessie is absolutely crazy about me.

CHAPTER

FIRST thing the next morning Jessie and I stopped by the *Tarmac* office. I had to finish typing the edited copy of my football article (Jessie complained that the first draft was "grossly overwritten"), and Jessie needed to gather together everything that was to be sent to the printer.

Just before the first period bell was due to ring, Lorraine Cassano stopped by to offer some help. Lorraine is a freckle-faced sophomore I had once considered dating — until I learned that her father was a dentist. I feel about dentists the same way that racehorses feel about the glue factory. I hope that I live out the rest of my life without ever meeting up with one. So the idea of dating a girl whose father actually made a living from torturing the mouths of innocent women and children was more than I could handle.

Jessie and I both had classes to catch, but Lorraine's first period was a study hall.

"So if there's anything else that needs to be done," she said, "I'd be more than happy to help out."

"That's really nice of you, Lorraine," said Jessie. "I've got a whole pile of stuff here that's waiting to be retyped and

16

proofread. And it all has to be ready for the printer by 3:00. I was going to ask Mr. Pearson if I could skip chemistry this morning to do it, but if you could get a lot of this out of the way now, I could probably finish up during lunch — which means I won't have to make up class time, which means I might actually have two or three minutes to myself to relax. Sounds just great to me! Lorraine, you're a lifesaver!"

"No problem at all, Jessie," she said. "My pleasure."

It even sounded like a good idea to me, so Jessie showed her what needed to be done and we both left for class.

When Jessie returned to the *Tarmac* office at lunchtime, she found that Lorraine had transformed the sloppy pile of barely legible, handwritten articles, notes, and letters to the editor into an impressive looking packet of neatly typed, grammatically correct, ready-for-the-printer copysheets. Jessie glanced over the first couple of items in the pile and satisfied herself that everything was in order. Lorraine had done everything Jessie had asked for and more. She seemed like a good person to have around.

Jessie stuffed the material into a large manila envelope and tucked it into an oversized three-ring binder. The printer was going to come by right after school to pick up the editorial packet, and Jessie was not going to let it out of her sight until it was safely in his hands.

Rick's warning had served its purpose. You could never be too careful.

CHAPTER

I WAS with Jessie when she received the message that Mr. Polansky wanted to see her and I agreed that it did seem a little unusual. There was a meeting of the *Tarmac* staff already scheduled for that afternoon, so if Mr. Polansky wanted to speak to her privately beforehand, it had to be about something important.

"But then again," I reasoned, "you're always getting overly dramatic about everything. Everything in your life is either a major catastrophe or the single greatest thing that's ever happened to any living creature." I shrugged my shoulders trying to look as casual as possible. "It's probably nothing."

I was wrong.

Two periods later, Jessie located me in the cafeteria. I had just worked up the courage to taste a revolting-looking glob of mush that the school menu had described as "Traditional Irish Stew" when Jessie sat down beside me and frantically yanked on my arm.

"Please, Lenny, I've got to talk to you." Jessie's face was swollen and blotchy and her hands were trembling. Her eyes were puffy and I could see that she had been crying.

She yanked on my arm again and led me outside to the courtyard. Most of the kids were still eating so we had the place pretty much to ourselves.

Jessie obviously had something to tell me, but she seemed to be struggling to find the right words. She kept choking on her words and blurting out incoherent phrases. I had seen her like this a few times before and I knew that the best thing to do was to simply wait patiently until she was ready to talk. After a couple of minutes, she finally spoke.

"That sneaky, no good, dirty, rotten, stinking, lousy creep!"

That was all she said. I waited a few moments expecting some sort of explanation, but none was offered.

"Mr. Polansky?" I finally asked in disbelief.

"No, stupid. *Lorraine.* Would you like to know what that little creep did? Well I'll tell you. No, better than that, I'll show you what she did."

With that statement Jessie flung open her notebook and removed a folded sheet of white paper. When she handed it to me I could see that it was a galley sheet from the *Tarmac* printer.

"Feast your eyes on this, dear brother," she said. "And if you ever tell me I'm getting overly dramatic again, I'm gonna clobber you over the head with a meat cleaver!"

I focused my eyes on the printed sheet and began reading:

BE A HIGH FLYER — LIGHT UP A JOINT

The time has come for the students and concerned faculty of Fairfield High School to take a firm stand on an issue of paramount importance in today's society — namely, the decriminalization of marijuana.

With volumes and volumes of research proving that marijuana is no more (and perhaps less) harmful than alcohol or cigarettes, it is a senseless and capricious miscarriage of justice to continue prosecuting law-abiding, tax-paying American citizens for the victimless crime of using marijuana in the privacy of their own homes. Something needs to be done, and it needs to be done now!

In an effort to protest this gross injustice, we are asking that all concerned students, faculty, and friends of Fairfield High School gather together on the steps of Town Hall on Friday, September 23, at 3:30 p.m. for a Marijuana Smoke-In.

Joints will be available for those individuals whose personal supply is currently depleted.

Jessica Marie Simpson
Editor-in-Chief

It took me a few moments before I even dared look at Jessie. I didn't know what to say.

"How? . . . I mean why? . . . When? . . . It just doesn't make any sense. . . . Surely, Mr. Polansky would never think . . . I mean, you would never . . . I mean . . . It's just unbelievable!"

"You took the words right out of my mouth," said Jessie.

She took back the galley sheet and hurriedly tucked it away inside her notebook.

"How did Mr. Polansky react?" I asked.

"How do you think? He was hardly jumping up and down for joy."

"Did you tell him it was Lorraine?"

"How could I? Even if I was sure it was her — and I

am — what could I do to prove it? Plus, it was partly my own fault anyway. I should have checked over everything before I sent it to the printer. That's the thing that Mr. Polansky was most angry about." Jessie shook her head slowly from side to side. She looked as sad as I had ever seen her. "He said he was very disappointed in me and hoped nothing like this would ever happen again."

We sat in silence for about five minutes, both of us trying to collect our thoughts. Jessie kept twirling her hair in tight little knots with her index finger, and I was fiddling with a dried twig, peeling the bark and snapping off smaller and smaller pieces. Jessie spoke first.

"Of course, it was Steve who was behind the whole thing."

Of course. It was the only possible explanation. By embarrassing Jessie in front of Mr. Polansky, Steve could reinforce his argument that he was really the better person for the job. The questionable part was what did Lorraine have to gain from it all. She was just one summer beyond being a timid and polite freshman, and now she had allowed herself to get involved in a reckless stunt where every finger of guilt pointed directly at her. The change in her could have resulted from only one thing, and just then we saw something that confirmed our suspicions. They were walking directly toward us, holding hands and gazing into each other's eyes like a pair of lovesick chipmunks. When they saw us they stopped briefly, and Lorraine stretched up onto her toes to whisper something in Steve's ear. They laughed and continued walking our way.

"Hi kids," said Steve with a broad grin. "How are my favorite little twins doing today?" Lorraine was holding onto his arm and giggling nervously.

"Listen, Steve," I said, "why don't you do me and the

rest of the world a big favor and get lost. And take your darling girl friend with you."

"Sure thing, old buddy," he said. He turned his eyes to Jessie and smiled with mock affection. "And don't forget about our date, cutie-pie — 3:30 on the steps of Town Hall. I'll be waiting for you."

He and Lorraine laughed their way across the courtyard and into the school building. Jessie and I stood up. Jessie straightened her skirt and ran her fingers through her hair. I brushed off my pants.

"No one can be that cruel," she said. "It's just not possible."

"Anything is possible," I said softly. "And if it's possible, you can be sure that eventually it's going to happen."

CHAPTER 7

THE next night Jessie, Rick, and I had a closed-door meeting in the *Tarmac* office. We had worked most of the day on the final editing and paste-up of the newspaper, and Jessie had personally delivered it into the hands of the printer. Every precaution had been taken to assure that there would be no more foul-ups like the Lorraine fiasco, but we were still worried.

"There's absolutely no doubt in my mind," said Rick. "The thing with Lorraine was only a trial run. Steve's planning something big and we'd better prepare ourselves."

Jessie agreed with Rick, and I agreed with both of them. So there we were, a picture-perfect trio of total agreement, but none of us knew what we could do.

"It's safe to assume that he's not going to try anything while the paper's at the printer. Even Steve's not that crazy," I said.

"Yeah, but that's not what I'm worried about," said Jessie. "It's when the paper arrives here that our problems are going to start."

We talked about some of the ways that Steve might try to sabotage the paper and readied ourselves for the worst.

We decided that one of us would oversee the delivery of the *Tarmac* from the printer, somebody else would make sure that the papers were securely locked inside the office, and we would all see to it that the distribution of the paper went smoothly and without interference from Steve or any of his trained gorillas.

None of it was necessary. The newspaper came back from the printer just the way it was sent out, looking neat, clean, and thoroughly professional. It was distributed during lunch period the following day and everyone seemed pleased with the result.

That afternoon there was a brief meeting of the *Tarmac* staff. Mr. Polansky congratulated us on a job well done. He shook hands with Jessie and Rick and told us to keep up the good work.

The whole operation had gone so well that for a moment we put Steve out of our minds. We figured that we had probably overestimated him, and it looked like clear sailing from there on.

That was our first mistake.

Our second mistake was checking the student activities board on the way home.

Steve's announcement was posted prominently in the middle of the bulletin board. It was hand-printed in giant-sized block letters on a large sheet of yellow construction paper, so you would have to be blind to miss it. Jessie and I read the announcement in dumbfounded amazement. Neither of us was able to talk, so we stood staring at the words until their meaning finally hit home.

WRITERS & ARTISTS

Tired of the Same Old Thing?
Make use of your creative talents and come join

us in the premier issue of the Fairfield High School LANDING STRIP, an exciting and thoroughly original alternative to our current student publications.

There will be an organizational meeting for all interested students at 3:15 in Room 227.

See you then.

Steven Braverman, Editor
Lorraine Cassano, Asst. Editor
Mr. Renaldo, Faculty Advisor

I put my arm around Jessie's shoulders.

The calm before the storm had just ended. A hurricane was on its way.

CHAPTER 8

"YOU can argue all you want, but my mind is made up," I said. "I'm going to that meeting tomorrow."

Jessie started to voice another objection but stopped herself when Rick started to stroke her hair. She rested her head upon his shoulder, comforted and reassured by his presence. My respect for Rick had quadrupled over the past week. He wasn't much of a talker, but when he spoke he usually made sense. Most important, he was a calming influence on both Jessie's lofty idealism ("Nobody can be that cruel.") and my desire for immediate and painful revenge ("I'd like to rip out his fingernails one by one."). He was the nicest guy that Jessie had ever dated and he was quickly becoming a good friend. The first was easy to accomplish, in view of the jerks that Jessie usually went out with, but the second was something that I never would have expected. It was a pleasant surprise.

"I think it's a great idea," said Rick, "but it has to be done right. You can't go in there waving your fist and shouting like a madman. That would turn off a lot of people, and right now we need all the friends we can get. You have to go as an observer, and unless you cause some kind of a wild scene, they wouldn't have any reason or any right to throw you out." Rick paused and fixed his eyes on mine. He looked as serious as my father. "Just try to stay reasonable."

"Does that mean I can't wear my 'Steve Braverman Has Leprosy' sweatshirt?" I asked.

"Correct," said Rick.

"Does it also mean that I can't bombard him with spitballs every time he tries to speak?"

"That's exactly what it means." Rick's expression was still deadly serious, but I could tell that he was trying hard not to smile.

"Well, can I at least make a motion at the meeting that Steve's official title be changed to 'editor-in-creep'?"

"Absolutely not," he said.

Actually what Rick said was closer to "absolutely nahhhhh." He never quite got out the final "t" before he started laughing.

"I just don't know about you, Rick," I said. "Sometimes you drive a really hard bargain."

CHAPTER 9

"HELLO, everybody. I'm Steve Braverman. It's good to see all of you here. I didn't realize I had quite so many fans."

There were about thirty students in the room and all but one of them laughed. I was the one who didn't.

"It's especially nice to see that the *Tarmac* has seen fit to send over one of their ace reporters to cover our little get-together." Steve pointed directly at me and I could feel everyone's eyes burning holes into my skin. "Would you like to stand up and take a bow, Lenny?"

I tightened my jaw and strained to remain calm. Despite the effort I could feel my face beginning to blush. A few underclassmen began to giggle, and I realized that I had to say something if I was ever to face any of these people again. I cleared my throat and took a deep breath.

"Cut the comedy, Steve, and get on with your business," I said. "I have every right to be here — especially since I seem to recall that you attended the first *Tarmac* meeting a couple of weeks ago."

I said this with a voice that was so steady that it even amazed me. The memory of his short-lived career with the

Tarmac caused Steve to lose his composure. He nervously shuffled his feet and then mumbled a reply.

"Okay, sure, everybody's welcome here, and uh, we've got a lot of work to do, so, uh, I guess we ought to get started."

Steve's stammering was making everyone uncomfortable, and I heard excited whispers coming from every corner of the room. Against my own wishes I actually began to feel sorry for him. But that only lasted for a moment. His natural obnoxiousness soon rose to the surface and he was his usual condescending, egotistical self again.

"I'd like to introduce Lorraine Cassano, our assistant editor, and Mr. Robert Renaldo, who has graciously agreed to serve as our faculty advisor. It was through Mr. Renaldo's assistance that we were able to secure a loan from the Student Council Activities Committee to help launch the *Landing Strip,* and I would like to express my sincere thanks to him."

That piece of information hit me in the gut like a runaway freight train. This was not kid stuff. Any thoughts I might have had that this was going to be a hastily-organized, poorly-planned, one-shot operation were quickly erased. Steve was not fooling around. He honestly wanted to replace the *Tarmac* with his own publication.

"Many of you are probably wondering why Fairfield even needs another newspaper. And I would have to agree with you that the *Tarmac* seems to do a decent enough job of reporting school activities and intramural sports results. They even list the weekly cafeteria menus. What more could you ask from a student newspaper?"

Steve paused briefly, smiled at Lorraine, and looked around the room as though waiting for someone to offer a suggestion.

29

"Well, to start with," he said, "you could ask that it be interesting. And entertaining. And timely. The *Tarmac* has been around since the turn of the century, and it really hasn't changed much since then. Because of this we feel that the time for an alternative student newspaper has come, and we've created the *Landing Strip* to fill that need. If you agree with our assessment of the situation, if you agree that we have a right to expect something more from our student publications, and if you feel that you have something to contribute to our effort, we'd like to invite you to join us in making the *Landing Strip* a successful and permanent feature of the Fairfield High community."

Steve went on to stress that the *Landing Strip* would serve as a showcase for the creative talents of its contributors. Originality would be encouraged, photographs and illustrations would make up a major part of the paper's format, and provocative journalism would be the rule rather than the exception.

"In short," said Steve, "we plan to publish a newspaper that will be as different from the *Tarmac* as the *Rolling Stone* is from *The New York Times.*"

Steve ended the meeting by passing around a sign-up sheet for interested students. He announced that the first editorial deadline would be at 3:00 the following Monday. Just about everybody in the room signed the list and Steve looked as pleased as a pig in a mud hole. Lorraine gave him an adoring smile and Mr. Renaldo patted him warmly on the back. The whole scene was making my stomach turn with anger and frustration so I hurried out the door.

"Lenny! Lenny, wait up a minute."

The voice was familiar, but for a moment I couldn't place it. I turned around and saw Rebecca pushing her way through a throng of students. She waved and smiled and my heart must have skipped about fifteen beats. Her hair was parted in the middle and pinned back just above her ears. She was wearing a frilly yellow blouse, brown corduroy jeans, and an embroidered suede vest. The combination was devastating. She looked like a cover girl from *Seventeen* magazine, and I had all I could do to stop myself from throwing my arms around her and declaring my eternal love.

"So what's your big hurry?" she said with a grin. "Got a heavy date or something?"

I shook my head, flapped my hands from side to side, and shrugged my shoulders. I did every stupid thing that people do when they can't think of an answer to a perfectly simple question. Since it was obvious that I was unable to coordinate my vocal cords with my brain waves, Rebecca took it upon herself to continue the conversation.

"I just wanted to tell you that I was impressed with the way you stood up to Steve at the beginning of the meeting."

Her words stopped me dead in my tracks. I stared at her with a look of total disbelief.

Rebecca was at the meeting? And I didn't notice her?

The thought was frightening — maybe even terrifying. There had to be something wrong with me. It didn't seem possible that I could have been in the same room with a girl as beautiful as Rebecca and not have noticed her. Such a mind-boggling thought made me stop and reconsider my priorities. Maybe I was taking this *Tarmac* stuff too seriously. I mean, after all, it is only a newspaper, while Rebecca is probably the single most exciting girl I've ever had the nerve to talk to. Maybe it was time for me to slow down and take a rest. Maybe it was time to ask Rebecca for a date.

"Are you okay, Lenny?"

Rebecca's voice snapped me back to attention.

"Oh, sure. I was just thinking about something. So what did you think of the meeting?"

"It sounds pretty interesting to me. I like things that are new and different." Her eyes were sparkling and she gave me a mischievous wink. "I showed some of my drawings to Steve before the meeting and he liked them, so I think I'll probably be doing some kind of a cartoon strip or something."

I nodded absently. This was not going to be easy. Half of me wanted to shout "Well, I hope you're out of a job real soon," while the other half wanted to congratulate her. Neither half won. I took the easy road.

"I didn't realize you were an artist," I said.

"Well, let's just say I'm trying to be," she said modestly.

We started walking down the hall. Rebecca stopped by her locker and took out a French phrase-book and a paperback copy of *The Great Gatsby*. She stuffed both of them into her oversized canvas pocketbook. All the while my insides were churning and my teeth were chattering so fast that I was afraid they would rip my tongue to shreds. I was dying to ask her out, but I didn't know how to do it.

"So tell me, Lenny," said Rebecca, "when are you and I ever going to get together outside of school? Are you busy this Saturday?"

My ears could not believe what they were hearing. I rapidly nodded yes, then realized that was the wrong answer and rapidly shook my head no.

"Well, how about taking in a movie with me? There's a Woody Allen film festival going on at the Schubert."

"That sounds fantastic," I said, blurting out the words. Since I wanted to have some input into the planning of this momentous occasion, I decided on the time. "I'll pick you up at 7:30, okay?"

"Perfect."

Rebecca smiled and ran down the hall to join a girl friend. I was beaming brighter than the newly risen sun, and I shouted a silent "Hooray!" inside my head.

I had done it. I actually had a date with Rebecca. And to think I had been worried. It couldn't have been easier.

CHAPTER 10

"I'VE been at Fairfield for thirty-seven years, and this is the worst thing that's ever happened here."

Mr. Polansky sat behind a heavily scratched oak desk that looked like it had been around the school for at least one hundred and thirty-seven years. He nervously tapped his fingers against the top of it. His face was pale and he seemed to be having difficulty catching his breath. He looked old, very old.

"And I can't put all the blame on Steven. He's basically a good boy. He's just upset and wants to do something to bolster his confidence and help him save face in front of his friends." Mr. Polansky paused and took a deep breath.

"In any event," he continued, "the *Tarmac* has competition for the first time in its history, and it is imperative that we work doubly hard to make sure that every issue is as good as we can possibly make it." Mr. Polansky hesitated as though debating whether or not to voice his next statement. He stared out the window and studied the fluttering leaves of a red maple tree. "I don't know about you," he said, "but I'm not about to give up without a whimper. If it's a fight they want, it's a fight they're going to get."

There was a momentary silence. Then:

"You can count on us," said Denise MacLean, the staff photographer.

"We're with you all the way," said Eddie Cartwright, our head sports writer.

Then there was a full chorus of agreement. We all whistled, slapped each other on the back and cheered for a couple of minutes. It was Rick who made us calm down and realize that all was not yet a bed of roses. We had a lot of work ahead of us.

"Up to now we've had a monopoly," he said. "Just about everybody in the school read the *Tarmac* simply because it was the only thing available. We had a captive audience, and there was no way we could lose. But now people have an alternative, and it's my guess that Fairfield is not big enough to support two newspapers. Students are going to have to make a choice between us and the *Landing Strip,* so we have to accept the fact that we're going to lose some readers. There's no getting away from that. The trick is to keep that number as small as possible."

"Very well put, Rick," said Mr. Polansky. "And the way to accomplish that, of course, is to turn out the better product. We have to write the best articles, take the best photographs, and do the best editing job imaginable. We have to be better than we've ever been before."

Jessie and I looked at each other. I managed a weak smile but Jessie only rolled her eyes with a sigh of frustration. I wondered if she was thinking the same thing I was. The meeting was beginning to sound more like a football team pep talk than an editorial jam session. All of this "Rah! Rah! We're Number One!" nonsense, which was supposed to be so inspiring, was only getting me down. It was nothing but cheap talk that wasn't getting us anywhere in a hurry. I leaned over to Jessie and held out my thumb like a microphone.

"And what do you think of all this, Ms. Simpson?" I whispered.

"I think I'd like to smash a typewriter over Steve's head," she said.

"Now, now," I chided, "haven't you been listening? The pen, dear sister, is mightier than the sword."

Jessie brushed back a stray hair and slowly ran her tongue over her lips.

"Yeah?" she said. "Well, sometimes I'd rather be a sword."

CHAPTER

I LOOKED forward to my Saturday night date with Rebecca with the same kind of anticipation that I used to reserve for Christmas, birthdays, and Little League games. I was sure it would be a night to remember.

Saturday morning I slept late and listened to a few oldie-but-goodie albums by the Beatles and Rolling Stones. I ate a leisurely lunch of hot dogs, baked beans, potato chips, and the most deliciously sour dill pickle that I have ever had the pleasure to experience. In the afternoon I played touch football with some of the neighborhood kids (needless to say, I am much too modest to mention the two touchdowns I scored to assist in my team's decisive 45–27 victory) and watched half of the National League playoff game on television.

I took my first shower at 5:00.

At 5:30 I ate dinner with the family. My mind was not on the meal and I hardly touched my plate. In my head I rehearsed all kinds of witty opening lines and humorous ad libs that I might be able to use during the evening. My brother, Andrew, made a few infantile remarks about my being lovesick, but I ignored him. Jessie and I went up to her room and listened to her favorite Paul McCartney album.

At 6:30 I took my second shower. I washed my hair, cleaned inside my ears, straightened my sideburns, and trimmed my fingernails. I spent about twenty minutes combing and blow-drying my hair. I put on a red-and-black checked flannel shirt and a pair of nicely faded, tight-fitting jeans. I brushed my teeth three times, gargled twice with a spearmint-flavored mouthwash, and dabbed a touch of Dad's aftershave on my neck, chin, and behind both ears. I was ready for anything and everything.

I hitched a ride to Rebecca's house from Bruce Lawson, our next-door neighbor. Bruce is a college freshman and a very handy guy to have around. The year before he had been the star pitcher of Fairfield's baseball team, and he was awarded a partial scholarship to the state university. During the spring and summer months, I usually spent a lot of time with him, playing catch to keep his arm in shape and futilely trying to hit his slow, looping curve ball. He was always willing to offer a few helpful hints on hitting or pitching to the kids in the neighborhood, and just about everybody liked him. Mom thought he was the perfect gentleman, and Jessie had a crush on him that was so severe she blushed with embarrassment every time he stepped into our yard. Dad and I both thought that he was simply a great guy. Needless to say, I much preferred having Bruce drive me to Rebecca's rather than Mom or Dad. Bruce would never do anything stupid to embarrass me, but with one of my parents I could never be sure.

Bruce left me off in front of Rebecca's house and playfully poked me on the shoulder.

"Give 'em hell, buddy," he said.

I grinned nervously and waved goodbye. I rang the doorbell and within five seconds was greeted by Mr. Weisberg, Rebecca's father. He told me that Rebecca was still getting ready and would be a few minutes longer. He led me into the living room and told me to take a seat. I had a choice between an expensive-looking crushed velvet sofa, a thickly cushioned armchair with leather upholstery, and a straight-backed rocking chair. I figured the rocking chair was my best bet. It looked the least expensive and the hardest to damage. I sat down, crossed my legs, looked around the room, uncrossed my legs, and looked around the room again.

Mr. Weisberg sat down on the leather armchair and smiled at me. He seemed to feel some kind of moral obligation to entertain me so we talked about the weather, the skyrocketing price of bottled soda, and a few other fascinating topics. He offered me a bowl of peanuts, and like a fool I almost reached for some. Luckily I regained my senses before making such a stupid mistake. I mean, after all, I had just brushed my teeth three times and gargled twice, so I was not going to let some salty little peanut do away with the springtime freshness of my breath. I had worked too long and too hard to throw it all away in the clutch. I would just have to be more careful.

After about ten minutes of mindless small talk with Mr. Weisberg, Rebecca finally made her grand entrance. As usual she looked terrific. She has a well-rounded figure, and she was wearing a pair of skin-tight white Levis and a cherry-colored denim blouse. I noticed that her father did not look too pleased with the way her pants clung to her legs and hips. I half expected him to say something, but he didn't — which was just fine with me. Rebecca kissed him on the cheek and promised to be home early. Mr. Weisberg and I shook hands, and he told us to have a good time. Then we were on our way.

Now it was up to me. A real, live, honest-to-goodness date with Rebecca was like a dream come true. I wanted it to be something special for both of us.

The theater was about half a mile from Rebecca's house. It was a beautifully ornate old building with a fancy lobby, crystal chandeliers, and two balconies. A lot of people thought it was a bit shabby compared to the ultra-modern theater at the shopping mall that had four different movie screens in the same building, but people have all kinds of crazy opinions, so I usually pay them little attention. In any event, the walk from Rebecca's house to the theater was just far enough to help us overcome the nervousness that people usually feel on a first date. We talked about how Rebecca was adjusting to a new town and a new school, and exchanged a few facts about our families and personal interests. Neither of us learned much that was new; rather, we were testing each other's reactions and trying to decide whether we really did get along as well as we seemed to. We did.

We arrived at the theater about fifteen minutes before the movie was to start so we sat together on a plush, gold brocade loveseat.

"Don't you just love this place?" said Rebecca. "It's absolutely gorgeous. Like something out of an old time movie."

Now that was one of those rhetorical questions that really can't be answered. I mean it was obvious that I agreed with her, but it would have been ridiculous to say "Yes, I agree with you." So I didn't say anything. Instead, I reached over and squeezed her hand with mine. She smiled and leaned her head upon my shoulder. Her hair was light and bouncy from our walk and it brushed softly against my eyes and cheeks. A few strands fluttered near my mouth, tickling my lips. I felt a very warm, very pleasant feeling flowing through my body, and I wished that everyone else in the theater would leave so I could kiss Rebecca for ten or twenty years without interruption. I was closer to being in love than I had ever been.

"You look beautiful tonight, Rebecca. Unbelievably beautiful." I had wanted to say that to her as soon as we left her house, but it would have sounded phony or rehearsed. At that particular time, however, it sounded like the most natural thing in the world.

"Thank you, Lenny, that's very sweet of you." Rebecca's words were spoken in a half-whisper that sounded as sexy as any Hollywood actress in any movie that's ever been made.

"You've probably heard that hundreds of times," I said.

Rebecca grinned and interlocked her fingers with mine.

"I haven't heard it nearly as often as you seem to think."

By this time, my combined states of excitement and nervousness had made me lose complete control of my already limited physical and mental faculties. My hands broke out in a cold, clammy sweat. My shoulder fell asleep and felt like someone was stabbing it with a thousand, razor sharp stickpins. My stomach began to gurgle and my legs began to twitch with very noticeable, but not at all rhythmic, muscle spasms. There was no way that my decidedly strange behavior could have escaped Rebecca's attention, but she gave no indication that she was disturbed by it. She was a treasure by anyone's standards.

Luckily, just as my body was about to totally humiliate me in front of Rebecca and a theater full of onlookers, the usher announced that the movie would be starting shortly.

Rebecca got up first and casually adjusted the waistband of her pants. I stood up beside her and for a few moments we looked into each other's eyes without speaking. It was so obvious that we shared the same feelings for each other that there was no need to say anything. We joined hands again and slowly walked into the theater. We chose a seat in the center section about halfway down the aisle.

To this day I have no idea at all what movie we saw, who was in it, or what it was about. Nonetheless, I loved every minute of it!

CHAPTER

"OH, HI, Lenny. How ya' doing? How did it go with Rebecca?"

Jessie's voice was kind of breathless and it was obvious that I had just interrupted Fairfield High's ideal couple in the middle of a hot and heavy make-out session. She and Rick were sitting on the living room couch watching the late evening news on television. Rick had his arms around Jessie's shoulders, and they both had their shoes off. The coffee table was littered with three or four empty Coke bottles, a box of pretzels, and one bag each of potato chips, corn chips, and pistachio nuts. Rick may be skinny but he can pack away a ton of food. Just about the only times I've seen him without something in his mouth were when he was talking or in situations like this when he was trying to put some moves on Jessie.

Not that I'm criticizing him or anything. I'm pretty much the same. I'm a perfect example of your basic, down-to-earth, all-American, junk-food junkie. And as far as Rick's trying to put some moves on his girl friend (even if she is my sister), well, all I can say is that my heart was totally on his side. After all, I had just returned from Rebecca's house, where I had enjoyed an unforgettable goodnight kiss that must certainly rank right up there among the world's all-time best kisses. With that experience fresh in my mind, I couldn't possibly disapprove of a little fooling around, no matter who was involved. Plus, I figure Jessie is old enough to take care of herself. She doesn't need me looking after her as if she were a little girl.

"We had a great time," I said. "A fantastic time."

I knew it would be thoughtless of me to stick around when they clearly wanted to be left alone so they could do what they were doing before I so rudely interrupted them, but I sat down anyway. I was flying higher than a 747 jetliner and I felt like talking to somebody. I was also hungrier than a two-hundred-foot-long tapeworm, and the lure of a junk food orgy was more than I could resist.

"So, lover boy," said Rick with a devilish grin that seemed grossly out of place on his innocent-looking face, "what did you get?"

I almost choked on that one. I had a mouthful of half-eaten, one-third-swallowed pistachio nuts and was in the process of washing it all down with a long sip of Coke. I started to laugh and had to press my lips together with all my strength to keep from spitting out the gloppy mixture. I forced myself to swallow but only managed to get it halfway down before I started to laugh again. I coughed and gagged and laughed and coughed again.

Jessie and Rick thought the scene was delightfully humorous and were rolling all over the couch in wild hysterics. Since I thought it was just as funny as they did, I could hardly get angry at them, so the three of us just sat there like complete fools laughing our heads off for about five minutes.

Rick's question is the all-time classic topic of conversa-

44

tion among high school guys (*and* among lots of high school girls, from what Jessie tells me), but the combination of his low-key delivery and the fact that Jessie was there made it sound like the funniest thing any of us had ever heard. Strangely enough, if Rick had asked me the same thing in a whisper when Jessie was not around, I probably would have told him — or at least made up something to tell him. I guess that doesn't say much for me, but I never claimed to be perfect. Wonderful, maybe, but not perfect.

"I can't even begin to tell you what a great time we had," I said when we all had finally stopped laughing.

"You really like her a lot, don't you?" asked Jessie.

"She's just fantastic," I said with a grin that must have stretched from ear to ear. "She's not like any other girl I've ever gone out with."

"Calm down, Lenny," said Rick. "She can't be that great or she'd never waste her time going out with you."

Jessie gave Rick a playful punch to the ribs and pushed him away when he tried to kiss her.

"Well, I think it's wonderful," she said. "And I'm really happy for you. I hope everything works out okay."

"Take it easy, Jess. I was only kidding," said Rick. "I have nothing against young romances — in fact, I rather enjoy them. I just don't think that people should get carried away after only one date."

"Why not?" argued Jessie. "You fell head over heels for me after our first date."

"Who are you kidding?" he joked. "You're the one who fell for me. I was practically an innocent bystander."

"Yeah, sure. Next thing you'll be telling me that you've got hundreds of girls chasing after your gorgeous body and I should be flattered that you even bother to give me the time of day."

"Thank you, Jessie," said Rick. "I couldn't have said it better myself."

Naturally, this mindless exchange ended with the two of them playfully wrestling and tickling each other. It wasn't very entertaining so I took the opportunity to stuff my face with handfuls of corn chips and gulps of soda (which, to be perfectly honest, were followed by some of the loudest burps that have ever been heard outside the locker room of the Fairfield High football team). I started to get interested in this weirdo science-fiction movie on TV, about a giant cockroach that was terrorizing the streets of Washington, and I completely tuned out the antics of Rick and Jessie. They must have been doing some pretty serious talking to each other, because just as the giant cockroach was preparing to attack the White House, Jessie started to clear her throat in that loud, obnoxious way that people use to attract somebody's attention. I ignored her as best I could, but she kept it up until I had no choice but to turn around and listen to her.

"First off," she said, "you know that I love you and I want nothing but the best for you. You're my brother and you're also one of my best friends. And, well, I just think that maybe Rick's right. Maybe you are rushing into this thing with Rebecca a little too fast."

"What's the matter with you two?" I shouted. I was starting to get angry and I could see that they were taken aback by the tone of my voice. "It's not like I'm running off tomorrow to marry the girl. We had a good time and I like her a lot. What's wrong with that?"

"There's nothing wrong with that," said Rick. "But there is potential for it to become a very sticky situation."

No matter what Rick said he sounded like someone

who was impersonating a lawyer. I usually got a kick out of it, but now it only made me angrier.

"*Every* situation has the potential to become sticky, but I'm not going to sit around and worry about problems that don't even exist."

"But that's the point, Lenny," said Jessie. "There is a problem that already exists — only you're purposely ignoring it."

"What problem?" I asked.

Jessie and Rick looked at each other woefully and shrugged their shoulders as if they couldn't believe I could be so dense.

"The fact of the matter," explained Rick in a fatherly tone, "is that our school is in the middle of a major confrontation. The *Tarmac* could very well be replaced by an offshoot newspaper that really has no right to even exist. I'm sure I don't have to remind you how disastrous that would be. Since the three of us are so deeply involved with keeping the *Tarmac* afloat, I think it's questionable whether you should allow yourself to get attached to someone who's working for the other side."

"The *other side?*" My voice was a shrill combination of anger and sarcasm. "Are we fighting a war or something?"

"You really should think about it," said Jessie. "We're not saying that you shouldn't go out with Rebecca ever again, but maybe you should slow down a little. At least until the situation with the newspaper cools off."

"I can't believe what I'm hearing," I said. "You sound like a couple of paranoid army generals. What are you so afraid of? Are you scared that I'm going to trade some top secret information for a lousy little kiss? I just can't believe this!"

"Look, Lenny, don't get all huffy," said Rick. "Just give it some thought. Steve is very sneaky and I wouldn't put anything past him."

"Oh, now I get it!" I exclaimed. "Now you think that Rebecca went out with me just to please Steve. You know, you really are nuts. The two of you, you're both crazy."

"Dammit, Lenny, would you just think about it," said Jessie. "Steve is a louse and he's liable to do anything."

"You really are scared, aren't you?" I asked.

"Cut the crap," said Rick. "We're not afraid of Steve. We're just trying to be careful."

"No, I don't think so. I think you are afraid. I think you're afraid of Steve, and I think you're afraid of what other people might think, and mostly I think you're afraid that the *Landing Strip* will turn out to be the better newspaper."

I stood up with a grand flourish that I admit was overly dramatic and headed up the stairs to my room.

Nobody said good-night.

CHAPTER 13

T HE next morning Jessie was all kinds of apologetic.

She knocked on my bedroom door at about 10:00 and asked if we could talk for a while. I was still lounging in bed, re-reading a week-old copy of *Sports Illustrated,* and I pretended to be uninterested in anything she could possibly say. She removed a pile of paperback novels and album covers from the top of a wooden orange crate that I use as a combination chair/endtable/junk box and sat down right beside me. She plopped her feet onto the bed and stared at me without blinking an eye for two or three minutes until I gave her my full attention.

"Mostly I want to say that I'm sorry for the way Rick and I acted last night. We had no right to try and interfere with your personal life. We were treating you like a child and we were wrong."

"Yeah, especially since you're the ones who were acting like children."

"Okay, Lenny. You don't have to get nasty. I get the point. You were right and I was wrong."

"And what's so unusual about that? It happens all the time."

"All the time, my ass," she said, kicking me on the shin. "It's happened about as often as it's snowed in July."

That remark set the tone of the rest of our conversation as we wandered off into a series of well-meaning insults. We were the best of friends once again.

It didn't go nearly as well with Rick.

I saw him for the first time during lunch period on Monday. I sat down opposite him and nodded hello. I took a bite of a rubbery hot dog, scooped up a forkful of dehydrated baked beans, ate a few soggy potato chips, and washed it all down with a gulp of imitation-chocolate-flavored milk. I made a mental note to send my compliments to the chef.

"So, good buddy," I said, "are you finally going to apologize for making an asshole of yourself Saturday night?"

"What for? I have nothing to apologize about."

"Come on, Rick. Don't you think this crap about Steve and Rebecca is a little crazy?"

"Not at all," he said. "And if I were you, I'd check into the situation before I started shooting off my mouth."

"You're really into this nonsense, aren't you?"

"First off, Lenny, it isn't nonsense. And I'm into it only because it's so obvious. You just have to open your eyes."

Rick pointed toward the far corner of the cafeteria, behind me and to my left, and motioned for me to turn around. I had no trouble picking out the scene he wanted me to observe. Seated together at a large round table were Steve, Lorraine, and Rebecca. The table was covered with sheets of paper that they were passing around and discussing. Occasionally they would jot down a few notes. They seemed to be having a great time together.

I was taken aback by what I saw but still not convinced. And I was determined to remain skeptical in the face of Rick's condescending self-righteousness.

"What's the big deal?" I asked. "They're just having lunch together."

"Somehow," said Rick with annoyance, "this seems to relate to our Saturday night conversation. I thought it might force some sense into that thick head of yours. I guess I was wrong."

"I'm not going to argue that Rebecca and Steve are not friends. But so what? It's not like he's a mass murderer or anything. He's just a stupid high school kid who happens to work for a student newspaper. He's not hurting anybody."

"What do you mean he's not hurting anybody? Jessie's been a nervous wreck lately. I can't concentrate on anything, and the *Tarmac* is in big trouble."

"And my dating Rebecca is the cause of all that?"

"Don't play the fool, Lenny — even if you do do it so well."

"Would you get off my back, Rick! You're starting to sound hysterical."

"And you're starting to sound like a love-sick fool who doesn't have enough sense to know he's being used."

I resisted the impulse to pound Rick across the face with my fists, and I resisted the urge to shower him with a colorful litany of swearwords, but I couldn't resist the temptation to somehow get even with him. So without saying a word in reply, I carefully removed the top of a pepper shaker and poured its contents into Rick's milk. I replaced the shaker top and grinned across the table.

"Now that was a very intelligent thing to do," said Rick. "Do you feel better now?"

"Not really," I said. "But I'm sure I will when I watch you drink your milk."

I raised my own glass to Rick in a mock toast and smiled my most innocent smile.

"Cheers," I said.

CHAPTER

THERE was no getting away from it. I had to talk to Rebecca myself, even if it only served to prove that Rick was right. The more I thought about it, the more likely it seemed that he actually could be right. Of course, I never would have admitted that to him.

I've never been a real whiz kid with girls, so naturally I felt flattered that a girl as beautiful as Rebecca would even consider going out with me. The thought that she might be dating me only to get information that might be useful to the *Landing Strip* gave me a sick feeling in the pit of my stomach. It made me angry and ashamed. I had to find out for myself. I had to talk to Rebecca and get everything out in the open.

I waited for her in the hall outside the cafeteria and reached for her hand as she drew near. I mumbled a hello and led her out to the courtyard. Her hand felt soft and warm, and I realized for the hundredth time that she was the best thing that had ever happened to me. I didn't want to lose her, but I also didn't want her to date me only because my sister was editor of the *Tarmac*.

We only had a few minutes before the bell rang, so I

had to be quick. My knees felt like overcooked spaghetti and my throat was painfully dry. I forced myself to talk, praying that I wouldn't hear anything I didn't want to know.

"I had a fantastic time Saturday night, Rebecca."

It was the kind of statement that led nowhere in a hurry, but it was a start.

"So did I," she said. "I hope we can do it again."

Rebecca smiled with an exuberance that brightened up her entire face.

"Well, that's sort of what I was getting at. I'd love to go out with you again, but I just want to be sure that there are no problems."

"Problems? What kind of problems?"

"Well, I'm not really talking about problems. I mean we don't have any problems right now, but there's the potential for problems, and I think we should try to stop them before they begin."

This was incredible. I was practically repeating Rick's warning word for word. Plus, to make it worse, I was making a fool of myself in front of Rebecca.

"What are you talking about, Lenny? If you'd rather not see me anymore, just say so. Don't talk gibberish."

"Of course I want to see you again. It's just that I'm a little confused. All this stuff with the *Tarmac* and the *Landing Strip* is driving me crazy."

"What's that got to do with us?" she asked.

"Maybe nothing, but I'd like to be sure."

"Sure about what? I honestly have no idea what you're talking about."

"Well, I mean I see you with Steve and Lorraine, and I know you're all good friends and it worries me. Steve would like nothing better than to embarrass Jessie in front of the whole school, and, well, she's my sister and I don't want her to get hurt. It wouldn't seem right for me to go out with someone who's trying to embarrass or hurt her. So I guess that's what I want to know."

"What is it that you want to know?"

"Come on, Rebecca. Don't make this any harder than it already is. I just want to know how involved you are with Steve and the rest of his gang."

"I don't know what's wrong with you, Lenny, but you sound like you've gone off the deep end. Once every couple of weeks I'm going to draw a few cartoons for a stupid school newspaper and you act like I'm committing murder or something. You're really acting weird. I mean, how would you feel if I accused you of dating me only to find out some dirt about Steve. Wouldn't that seem ridiculous to you?"

Rebecca's voice had grown a lot louder, and half the kids in the courtyard were looking over at us to see what the fuss was about.

"Okay. Don't get so excited. Maybe I am overreacting. But I care about Jessie a lot, and I care about you a lot, and I just don't want anything to get screwed up."

"Then don't worry about it so much or else *you're* the one who's going to screw it up."

"Yeah, I guess you're right." I placed my hand on Rebecca's shoulder and ran my fingers along the base of her neck. "So would you like to go out for a bite to eat after school?"

"I can't," she said. "I promised Steve I'd help out with the proofreading."

The mention of Steve's name made me tense up, but Rebecca sensed my reaction and put her arm around my waist.

"How 'bout if we get together on Friday night?" she

asked. "Bonnie Jackson's having a party. It should be a lot of fun."

"I guess so," I said. It sounded like a good time but I couldn't muster very much enthusiasm.

The bell rang for the next period, and we headed into the building. Rebecca had a chemistry class on the second floor, and I watched her climb the stairs. She was wearing a denim skirt and her legs looked long and graceful as they glided from step to step.

Going out with Rebecca was probably going to be one hassle after another, at least as long as this newspaper business continued, but she was definitely worth it. There was no doubt about that.

CHAPTER

"THIS is not a newspaper! It's nothing but garbage. It's a disgrace!"

Mr. Polansky was angry, Jessie was angry, Rick was angry, and just about everyone else on the *Tarmac* staff was angry. I was, too, but mostly I was amused. I couldn't understand what all the fuss was about.

It was Friday and the first issue of the *Landing Strip* had just been published. Its maiden appearance was a typical Steve Braverman production with lots of noise and fanfare.

Midway through lunch period, Steve, Lorraine, and a half dozen or so other *Landing Strip* staff members marched into the cafeteria. Steve led the way, and with his arms held up high over his head, he proudly displayed the front page of his newly-born brainchild. He was smiling brightly in the obnoxious way that was his trademark. Three of his assistants were carrying instruments — a guitar, a clarinet, and a snare drum — and were playing an up-tempo version of the Fairfield High fight song, while others in the group handed out sample copies of the newspaper. Steve halted the procession in the center of the room and stepped up on a chair. He gave a thoroughly forgettable speech full of clichés and overstatements that I will refrain from quoting to spare everyone an unnecessary attack of nausea.

The full-scale distribution of the *Landing Strip* took place during final homeroom period, so everyone on the *Tarmac* staff had a chance to look it over before our afternoon meeting. As a result, the meeting was not a very joyful occasion. The atmosphere in the room was a cross between a funeral and a Hell's Angels' reunion: Sadness mixed with anger. All in all, it did not make for a good time. I was tempted to leave, but I figured it had to get better. As usual, I was wrong.

Mostly it was the style and tone of the *Landing Strip* that was getting everyone all hot and bothered. As Steve had said at the newspaper's first organizational meeting, he intended for the *Landing Strip* to be as different from the *Tarmac* as the *Rolling Stone* was from *The New York Times*. He was true to his word. Steve's reporters wrote in a very personalized, anecdotal way that went far beyond the style-less formula of who-what-when-where-why-and-how. The problem, as Mr. Polansky saw it, was that they were not being educated as journalists and too often they failed to even mention the who-what-when-where-why-and-how of a story. Mr. Polansky probably blamed Mr. Renaldo for that; the rest of us blamed Steve.

As for the content of the *Landing Strip,* it was half traditional and half radical. It had all the standard high school newspaper articles about pass-fail grading systems, more elective courses, recaps of team sports, and previews of upcoming student activities. But it also had another variety of writing that was never seen in the *Tarmac*. There were, in fact, a few pieces that struck me as being a bit much.

Lorraine's byline was listed above a lengthy article that discussed the biorhythm cycles of about twenty teachers.

Using their birthdays as a starting point, Lorraine claimed to have compiled accurate biorhythm charts for each of them. She then proceeded to outline the personality characteristics and potential "good days" and "bad days" for each teacher. Lorraine ended the piece with a firm promise to expand her study to include every teacher in the school as well as the principal, guidance counselors, and driving instructor.

There was also an article by Bob "Bobo" Lankitas listing half-a-dozen local bars and taverns that were very lenient about checking ID's of possibly underage customers. Bobo was a senior track and field star who had earned a school-wide reputation as a ladies' man because of a totally unproven rumor that he had once dated a twenty-year-old divorcée. I never thought highly of Bobo in the first place and my estimation of him dropped about thirty points after reading his article. Nonetheless, I did copy down the names and addresses of two of the bars he mentioned. Just in case.

The article that seemed to upset Jessie the most was a blatant parody of a regular *Tarmac* feature called "The Alumni Corner." The *Landing Strip* version was called "Alumni Forum." The names were similar but the content couldn't have been more different. Jessie wrote most of the alumni pieces for the *Tarmac,* and she would usually single out an outstanding graduate of Fairfield who had gone on to fame and fortune. The kinds of people the *Tarmac* wrote about were doctors, lawyers, teachers, and business leaders who followed the traditional routes of success — namely, college and hard work. Not so with the *Landing Strip* version. Margaret Saunders, a shy sophomore who hardly said a word but put everyone to shame on the dance floor, wrote a rambling piece on Satch MacKenzie, Class of '76. Satch had been Student Council president during his senior year at

Fairfield and had gone on to Princeton. His first year at college went well, but as a sophomore he began feeling "oppressed" by the rigidity of the academic world and dropped out. He formed a punk rock group and authored such memorable songs as "Disco Death," "My Baby Left Me So I'm Gonna Leave You," and "Boom Boom, Bam Bam." His musical taste was not savored by a very large audience, so he left the music world for the challenges of dishwashing and unemployment. He was now selling magazine subscriptions door-to-door and trying to save enough money to buy a customized moped. Margaret's article about Satch was certainly interesting (although I would probably be the only *Tarmac* staffer to admit it), but he definitely was not the type of person anyone would hold up as a role model. He was an out-and-out flake, which is probably why Steve decided to assign an article about him. Flakes are a lot like bananas — they tend to hang around together.

Still, I couldn't understand why everyone was so upset. This kind of journalism was exactly what everyone should have expected from Steve.

Midway through the meeting, with everyone hollering back and forth about how awful the *Landing Strip* was, I finally figured out what they were all afraid of. It didn't seem like anyone else was going to say it, so I took it upon myself.

"The thing I would like to know," I said, "is why you're all beating around the bush? No one's going to deny the fact that the *Landing Strip* could use some improvement. It leaves a lot to be desired no matter how you look at it. But that's nothing to get angry about. And it's certainly nothing to be worried about. Unless, of course, that's not really what's bothering you."

I quickly scanned the room trying to catch everyone's eyes in the process.

"What's that supposed to mean?" asked Rick with a healthy dose of irritation in his voice.

"It means that if the *Landing Strip* is so terrible, we should all be thrilled, because it'll just die off and we'll never hear from it again."

Rick let out a big sigh of exasperation and rolled his eyes with a "Who's gonna shut this guy up?" expression.

"Of course," I continued, "maybe the truth of the matter is that the *Landing Strip* isn't really that bad. Maybe it's only different. And maybe, because it is a little different, it's going to be more popular than anything the *Tarmac* can offer."

"That's a lot of maybe's, Lenny," said Jessie.

I should have figured that Jessie would be the first to take issue with me. I didn't relish the thought of arguing with her, and I didn't want to say anything to hurt her. But I also didn't feel it was right to let the charade continue.

"Well, if you want," I said, "you can take out the 'maybe' in every statement I've made, and I'll still stand behind each one."

"What are you trying to say?" asked Rick. "That we should cover our faces with smiles and throw a big celebration party for Steve and his friends?"

"Yeah, Lenny," said Eddie Cartwright, "don't you think we have a right to be angry?"

"No, I really don't."

"You don't?" asked Mr. Polansky.

For a while I had forgotten that Mr. Polansky was even present. The sound of his voice was an immediate reminder that my every word was being carefully analyzed and considered, so I had better make them good.

"No, Mr. Polansky. We had a time to be angry when Steve first organized the *Landing Strip*, but that time is past.

We've known for weeks now that he was going to publish another paper, so we shouldn't be angry simply because he's done what he said he would do. And we most certainly shouldn't be angry that the quality of the paper is not as good as the *Tarmac.*"

"How would you like us to react, Leonard?" asked Mr. Polansky.

"To start with," I replied, "I think we should consider the good points of the *Landing Strip*. From what I could gather from listening to the reactions of kids in the cafeteria and halls, Steve's paper is going to find a large audience. The writing may not win any prizes, but it's lively, the graphics are well done, and the headlines catch your eye whether you want them to or not. I have a hunch it's going to become the most popular thing that's happened to Fairfield in years."

"If you love it so much," said Rick, "why don't you go on over and enlist? I'm sure Steve would welcome you with open arms."

Rick let out a hollow laugh and glanced around the room searching for approval. I noticed that about half of those present nodded in agreement.

"Enough of that, Rick," said Mr. Polansky. "Leonard is free to speak his opinion and you're free to disagree, but I won't stand for any childish taunts."

That quieted Rick in a hurry. He blushed a bright pink and lowered his eyes sheepishly.

"But what exactly *are* you saying, Lenny?" asked Jessie. "If you can't beat 'em, join 'em?"

"No, but I don't think there's anything wrong with a newspaper being fun to read. That doesn't mean that it has to be bad. Maybe we could come up with a happy medium. We wouldn't have to lower our standards."

62

"But that's exactly what would happen," said Jessie. "The *Tarmac* would never be the same. And I'm not going to be the editor who lets it go down the drain."

I shook my head slowly from side to side. I started to protest but stopped myself. Jessie was my sister, and I cared about her. I didn't want to fight with her — especially in public. I leaned back in my chair and folded my arms across my chest. It was clear to everyone that I had spoken my piece and had nothing more to say.

Unfortunately, the same could not be said for the rest of the gathering, and the meeting dragged on for another half hour. When it was over everybody was still angry.

I, however, was no longer amused.

CHAPTER 16

LOOKING back, I realize that the situation could have been a lot worse. For one thing, Rebecca's contribution to the *Landing Strip*'s first issue was rather minimal — about a half dozen pen and ink sketches — and not at all controversial. As a result, I did not have to listen to the combined ranting and raving of Jessie and Rick about how I was being used by a seductive enemy agent. It also helped to put my own mind at ease.

For another, Jessie was not holding a grudge against me because of my behavior at the *Tarmac* meeting. Jessie got home first that afternoon, and when I arrived she greeted me as though nothing at all had happened. We went upstairs to her room, shared a pre-dinner snack of apple juice and corn chips, and listened to a couple of albums. Jessie showed me the first draft of an editorial she was writing that advocated more in-class use of audio-visual materials. I offered a few editorial suggestions, some of which she ignored as being "absurd" and some which she incorporated into the piece. We spent a very nice hour together — one of the nicest times we had shared for almost a month. By the time Mom called us down for dinner the hassles of the afternoon seemed ages away.

After dinner both Jessie and I set about preparing ourselves for the party at Bonnie Jackson's house. I did about twenty minutes of calisthenics — pushups, situps, jumping jacks, and deep knee bends — and then hopped into a steamy shower. Just before I finished, I turned off the hot water and turned on the cold full force. I could only stand it for about ten to fifteen seconds, but it was enough to perk up every cell in my body. It was a delightful torture that gave me goose bumps in places where I didn't even know I had places.

When I finished dressing, I knocked on Jessie's door to tell her I was leaving. The party at Bonnie's was a big thing, and it seemed like everybody in the school was going. Bonnie had asked people to start coming at 8:30, but I told Rebecca I'd pick her up about a half hour earlier. That way we would have a little time together just by ourselves. Jessie said that she and Rick were going to be a little late, but they would look for us when they arrived.

Rebecca opened her front door before I even had a chance to ring the bell. She explained that her parents had gone out for dinner and she was the only one home.

"They made me promise that I wouldn't let you in the house," she said with a giggle. "After all, what would the neighbors think?"

"Don't your parents trust me?" I asked, hoping with all my heart that they didn't. I couldn't imagine anything I'd like better than for a girl's parents to think that I was a supercool, hotstuff lover who was about to sweep their daughter right off her feet.

"Of course they do," replied Rebecca. "It's me they're worried about."

Rebecca threw back her hair in the flirtatious way that television actresses do in shampoo ads. She took hold of my hand and we began walking slowly toward Bonnie's house.

"So what do you think?" she asked.

"What do I think about what?" I honestly didn't know what she was getting at.

"What do you think about the *Landing Strip*? It's pretty good, huh?"

This was the one topic that I had hoped would not come up. Since it had, I wanted to be done with it as quickly as possible.

"Well, I wouldn't exactly recommend that you hold your breath until it gets nominated for a Pulitzer."

"Don't be a wise guy," she said. "I just asked if you thought it was good. I *know* it isn't great."

"To be perfectly honest, Rebecca, I'm not all that thrilled with it. I thought your sketches were terrific, but a lot of the writing was pretty bad."

I didn't want to admit to Rebecca that I thought the *Tarmac* could improve a bit by adopting some aspects of the *Landing Strip*'s low-key style. But I especially didn't want the tenor of this conversation to put a damper on the rest of our evening.

"It's no worse than a lot of the junk the *Tarmac* prints. Most of it's a lot better."

If the conversation continued to progress along these lines, there would not even be a "rest of the evening." Luckily I came up with a plan. I had seen Cary Grant in the same sort of situation in a 1940's movie, and he had handled it with perfect aplomb. I figured if it worked for him it would probably work for me.

I turned to Rebecca and took both her hands in mine.

I kissed her lips ever so lightly, leaned back and smiled lovingly, then kissed her again.

"It really doesn't matter which one of us is right," I said. "You have your opinion and I have mine, and nothing is going to change either of our minds. So let's just forget it and enjoy ourselves."

I doubt that my delivery sounded as smooth as Cary Grant's, but I know it sounded just as sincere. Rebecca fell for it hook, line, and sinker. She hugged me tightly and brushed her lips against my cheek. We stood silently for a few moments, alternately hugging and gazing into each other's eyes. It was a magical kind of moment.

Too bad magical moments can't last forever.

CHAPTER

WE COULD hear Bonnie's party from two blocks away. The stereo was blasting, and as we walked up the sidewalk to the front door, we could see the bouncing silhouettes of kids dancing in the living room. A cute, freckle-faced girl who introduced herself as Bonnie's sister, Louise, let us into the house. Louise looked about fourteen years old. (Actually, she looked like a twelve-year-old trying to look like a sixteen-year-old.) She was wearing Indian jewelry, denim pants, and a flowery blouse that were all obvious hand-me-downs from Bonnie. I wanted to tell her to enjoy being fourteen before she worried about being older, but it wouldn't have had any effect. Besides, Jessie and I were the same way when we were her age, and we both turned out okay.

"Hi, Lenny, good buddy! How ya' doing?"

Butch Cochran pounded me on the back in his own inimical way. Butch is about 6′ 2″ and close to two hundred pounds. He looks like the kind of guy who would be a star athlete in football, boxing, wrestling, and track. He is. He's also a little on the dumb side, but I try not to let that bother me. He's a good person to have as a friend.

Rebecca and I followed Butch to the downstairs family room, where a giant fire was roaring in the fireplace. Bonnie had arranged for her older brother to buy a few cases of beer, so just about everybody was drinking and dancing and laughing up a storm. It was the first time I had ever danced with Rebecca, and I was pleased to discover that we were well matched on the dance floor. Once in a while we would switch partners for a fast dance, but we always reserved the slow numbers for each other.

Jessie and Rick got to the party at about 9:30 and quickly joined in with our group. Butch did a hilarious impersonation of how his father had tried to explain the facts of life to him. Eddie Cartwright told some really poor "dead baby" jokes. His girl friend, Cyrisse, sang a couple of obscene songs she had learned from her married sister. Rick was quiet at first, but after a few drinks he began entertaining us by juggling — or attempting to juggle — three empty beer bottles.

Crash!

Splat!

Silence.

Rick discovered that juggling was not nearly as easy as it looked. Two of the three bottles crashed to the floor and shattered into a hundred tiny pieces. The third was spared only through a miracle: It flew over Rick's shoulder and landed in the lap of Theresa Owens. Theresa was at that moment making out with her boyfriend, Jim Something-or-other, and she assumed that the bottle was actually Jim's hand trying to get fresh with her. She leaned back and slapped him across the face with all her might. The poor guy never had a chance.

"That's very good, Rick. If you'd like to do it again, I'll get one of my photographers down here."

The voice was sneering, condescending, and scornful. It could only be Steve Braverman.

"Why not?" said Rick. "The more pictures you use, the less crap there'll be to read in that rag of yours."

Steve arched his eyebrows and tilted his head slightly as though surprised that Rick could have come back with such a clever retort.

"If you're referring to the *Landing Strip*," he said, "I think we've already established how interesting we can be. Just ask anyone here tonight. Anyone, that is, who's not connected with the syrupy-sweet *Tarmac*."

Everyone had stopped dancing and the music was lowered. Kids from the rest of the house crowded into the doorway to catch a glimpse of the goings-on.

"Don't kid yourself, Steve," said Jessie. "You've got a long way to go to catch up with the *Tarmac*. One lousy issue — and I do mean *lousy* — doesn't mean a thing."

"It won't take long," said Steve. "Wait and see. It's not going to take long at all." Steve took an exaggerated gulp of beer and drained the bottle. He shook it slowly from side to side to show everyone it was empty. "See you later, kids. I think I'll get myself another drink."

Steve left the room. At first it was quiet, but after a few minutes of excited whisperings, the party came back to life.

The same could not be said of Jessie.

There had been something ominous in Steve's words. He definitely had a few more tricks up his sleeve, and lately he seemed to be turning into a master magician.

I just wished he would do the best trick of all and make himself disappear.

CHAPTER

I T WAS 3:45 on Monday afternoon — fifteen minutes past the editorial deadline for the *Tarmac*'s next issue.

"I don't understand it," said Jessie. "None of these people has *ever* been late with an article before."

"They probably just forgot about the deadline," suggested Rick. "How 'bout if I try calling a couple of them at home?"

"That sounds good. If we have to, we can always pick up their articles on the way home."

Rick left the room to place his phone calls. I stayed in the *Tarmac* office with Jessie, Eddie Cartwright, and Denise MacLean, the staff photographer. While Jessie and Denise looked over a group of photographs and discussed which ones would make the best illustrations, Eddie and I stretched out and took it easy.

"How did you feel Saturday morning after the party?" he asked.

"My head was a little woozy, but it really wasn't bad at all. I've had worse hangovers, that's for sure."

Eddie nodded and smiled knowingly.

Actually, I was lying through my teeth, but Eddie had

no way of knowing that. I can really throw the bull when I want to. I hardly ever drink, and when I do I don't drink very much. So, in reality, I've never been cursed with the pains of a hangover. But I didn't want to admit that. Practically every conversation in the men's room, courtyard, or locker room on Monday morning revolves around how much you drank or how far you got with your girl friend over the weekend. I never went out of my way to make up stories to tell the guys, but if someone asks me, I'm not always as truthful as old Honest Abe would want me to be.

"How long have you been going out with Rebecca?"

"A few weeks now."

"She's really something. One of the prettiest girls I've ever seen. I'll tell you, Lenny, if I ever had a chance with a girl like her, I'd hold on so tight you'd need the entire backfield of the Los Angeles Rams to get her away from me."

My reply came in the form of a smile. As far as I was concerned — and with Rebecca's continued cooperation — there was no way I was going to let her get away. I hate sad stories and I most definitely did not want to be featured in one with Rebecca as my co-star.

Jessie called us over to the desk where she and Denise were working. Eddie had written an article on the progress of the football season, and Jessie wanted him to choose between two possible illustrations. One of them showed our quarterback tossing a lateral pass to his tight end, while the other showed the opposing team's halfback being smothered by three Fairfield linemen.

"I really can't make up my mind," said Eddie. "They're both great."

"Okay," said Jessie. "That settles it. We're just going to have to use both of them."

"Next time, Denise," I said, "do us a favor and take a few crummy pictures. I hate to see my sister's hair turn gray with all these difficult decisions."

Jessie glanced at me with a cheerful smile, but her eyes moved past me and her expression suddenly hardened. I followed her gaze: Rick was standing in the doorway. He looked like someone who would rather be anywhere than where he was. He was definitely the bearer of bad news.

"What's the matter, Rick? What happened?"

"He's really done it to us this time," said Rick.

No one had to ask who Rick was talking about. The next chapter in the continuing saga of "Steve 'The Creep' Braverman Fights Back" had just begun.

"I'm afraid to ask, but what did he do?" asked Jessie.

"Well, it's no coincidence that six of our reporters just happened to forget about the deadline all at the same time. Steve had more than a little to do with it."

"How?" asked Jessie. Her voice was starting to panic. "Would you please tell me what he did?"

"I guess you could say that he made them an offer they couldn't refuse."

"You don't mean . . . ?"

"Yep. Our six forgetful reporters are now working for Steve, and the articles you assigned them will be their first contributions to the *Landing Strip*."

"They can't get away with that," shouted Jessie. "We won't let them. I won't let them."

"There's really nothing we can do about it. They wrote the articles and they can do anything they want with them."

"I was afraid something like this was going to happen," said Eddie. "I had a feeling."

"Why didn't you tell us then, Eddie? At least we could have prepared ourselves," said Jessie.

"I guess I was scared. And a little ashamed. Steve approached me a couple of days ago and asked if I would consider becoming his sports editor. He said my byline would be given a lot more prominence, and he hinted that maybe I could take over for him next year when he graduates. I told him to screw off, of course, but I should have figured he would also be talking to other *Tarmac* people." Eddie paused and let out a deep sigh. "I'm sorry, Jess. I should have said something."

He was looking pretty miserable so I patted him on the shoulder for comfort.

"Forget it, Eddie," said Jessie. "You had no way of knowing what Steve was up to."

"And even if we had known, I don't know what we could have done about it anyway," said Rick.

"That's true," agreed Jessie. "And now that it's done I still don't know what to do."

"Maybe it would help if you talked to some of these kids personally, Jessie. Maybe they would listen to you," suggested Denise.

"Absolutely not. I'm not going to beg the little creeps to come back. If they can be swayed that easily by Steve's crap, I'd rather not even have them around here."

"Then what are we going to do," Rick asked. "If we don't get all our copy to the printer by tomorrow afternoon, we'll never get the paper published on schedule, and that's only going to make us look bad in everyone's eyes."

"There's no question about that," said Jessie. "We've got to have the paper ready by tomorrow. And if we have to stay up all night working on it, well, that's all right with me."

The rest of us voiced our unanimous approval for Jessie's sentiments. It was too soon for us to roll over and play dead. And while I sometimes questioned treating the

74

Landing Strip as though it were our mortal enemy, the underhanded tactics of this last move rekindled my lifelong desire to shove a hockey puck down Steve's throat. I decided right then and there to forget about my previous misgivings and devote myself wholeheartedly to putting both Steve and his *Landing Strip* out of business. I knew it would be difficult to accomplish, but it made me feel better just to think about it.

In some ways it's very helpful to have someone as detestable as Steve around to constantly struggle against. It brings out the best in us good guys and gives us a goal to work toward. And even a crazy goal like mine is better than no goal at all.

The image in my mind of Steve Braverman choking on an oversized hockey puck was enough to keep me working for three days and nights without food or water. It gave me a feeling comparable to the joy I felt the first time I ate strawberry shortcake.

"Let's get to work," I said with heartfelt enthusiasm. "We've got a big job ahead of us."

CHAPTER 9

"**Y**OU did an excellent job," said Mr. Polansky. "And under the worst possible circumstances. I'm very proud of you."

He was right. We had done a great job. Jessie had been determined to have the *Tarmac* published complete and intact, and she had instilled us all with that determination. She asked each of us — Rick, Eddie, Denise, and me — to write an article of about six hundred words on any school-related topic that interested us. She also went through the paper's editorial file and came up with three other manuscripts that were being held for editing and revision. Hers was a time-consuming project that she finally completed at 2:30 in the morning. In all, we managed to fill the gaps left by the defection of our turncoat reporters with a surprisingly high quality of writing. The paper was published on schedule, and no one would have been able to guess how close we had come to disaster.

"As for the guerrilla warfare tactics of the *Landing Strip*," continued Mr. Polansky, "I am completely disgusted. I have discussed the situation with everyone from the principal to the president of the P.T.A. to Mr. Renaldo himself; but nothing has yet been resolved to my satisfaction. I want to assure you, however, that I will not let the matter drop. The whole affair makes my blood boil."

Mr. Polansky was really worked up. His face was beet red and the veins on his neck bulged out with the strain of his anger. He looked like he wanted to throw something — or someone — against the wall but knew that he shouldn't. I knew just how he felt. There's nothing worse than the frustration that comes from being unable to vent your anger. Usually it's because there's someone else around who will chastise you for acting like a child or else give some stupid advice like "Two wrongs don't make a right." In Mr. Polansky's case, he was probably held back by his sense of professional responsibility; in my case, it's usually my parents.

Jessie stood up in front of the small gathering and pressed her palms together in a serious pose.

"I'm sure this is going to sound trite and maybe even a little melodramatic," she said. "But it's at times like these when you learn who your friends really are. And, well, I just want to thank all of you for being my friends and standing with me."

Practically everybody in the room responded with a little embarrassment, nodding their heads and shrugging their shoulders with an "Aw, shucks" expression. There was also a lot of mutual affection in the air, and more than one person looked a little misty-eyed.

After the meeting Jessie, Rick, and I stopped by the auditorium to watch the auditions for a student theater production of *Grease*. The girls had teased hair and were dressed in bobby socks and cashmere sweaters. The boys were wearing tight black pants and leather jackets, and each had slicked-back hair that looked like it had been dipped in an engine crankcase. All the kids looked pretty ridiculous, but I had to give them credit just for having the nerve to get up on stage. I know I could never do it.

Rick left early, saying he had to finish reading *The Catcher in the Rye* for English. Jessie and I hung around the auditorium a little longer and then slowly walked down the hallway to our lockers. I had gym class that morning, and the two or three quarts of sweat that had been absorbed by my tee shirt, shorts, socks, and sneakers made my locker smell like decaying gefilte fish. Jessie pretended to faint from the odor while I inhaled deeply, exaggerating my pleasure while doing my best not to gag.

"Ah!" I exclaimed, stretching my arms toward the foul-smelling gym bag. "There's nothing like the clean, crisp smell of the outdoors to make you feel alive."

"Or make you wish you were dead," said Jessie.

We stopped by Jessie's locker to retrieve her chemistry notebook and a couple of paperback novels she had borrowed from the school library. We were both in good spirits as we trotted out the side entrance of the school and headed across the parking lot. We should have known that our sense of well-being would be short-lived. Our bubble was burst by the sudden appearance of Steve, Lorraine, and a few other *Landing Strip* writers.

"Well, speak of the devil," said Steve. "If it isn't our good friends Leonard and Jessica, Fairfield High's answer to the Bobbsey Twins. How are you kids doing today?"

"Pretty good up till now," said Jessie.

"Hey! Don't get so uptight. We're all friends here. Why don't we just let bygones be bygones," said Steve.

"Go sell your crap to somebody else," I said, "because I'm not gonna buy it."

I had come to a point in my relationship with Steve

where I could only stand him in doses of two or three seconds. Having to deal with him for a period longer than that strained my patience to the breaking point.

"You are truly hurting me, Lenny," said Steve with mock sadness in his voice. He pressed his hands against his chest as though his heart were about to break. "But just to prove that there are no hard feelings on my part, I'm going to give you and your cute little sister an opportunity to help propel Fairfield High into the twentieth century."

Steve unclasped the oversized manila envelope he was carrying and pulled out a handful of papers. He handed one to Jessie and told us to read it. The paper was set up in a petition format, with a brief opening statement and a line of numbered spaces where people could sign their names.

We read in disbelieving silence:

> Whereas the *Landing Strip* has proved to be more responsive to the needs and likes of the Fairfield student body,
>
> And whereas the *Tarmac* has neglected its duty to keep pace with the progress and tenor of both the school and contemporary society,
>
> We, the undersigned, support the petition of the *Landing Strip's* executive board that the *Landing Strip* be recognized as the official student newspaper of Fairfield High School.

If I'd had a gun I would have shot him.

If I'd had a knife I would have cut him up into a thousand little pieces.

All I had were my fists, and I gave him a shot to the stomach that I know neither of us will ever forget. I knocked the wind out of him and jumped on his back as he started to fall to the ground. He steadied himself on one knee and rammed his elbow into my kidneys. For a moment the pain was so intense that I thought I was going to throw up. We both landed a few more weak punches and cursed each other from heaven to hell and everywhere in between. We were both barely able to breathe and totally unable to struggle against the efforts to separate us.

We stood about ten feet apart, huffing and puffing, glaring at each other with undisguised hatred in our eyes. Lorraine and Jessie stood between us forming a protective buffer zone. My nose was bleeding and I hurt all over. Steve was clutching his ribs and he leaned against Lorraine for balance. He looked like he was in severe pain, and I'm not at all ashamed to admit that the sight of his suffering filled me with joy. I wanted to hurt him physically as badly as he had hurt Jessie emotionally, and I had succeeded.

There's nothing like success to help heal the wounds of battle.

Jessie took my arm and we turned our backs on Steve and his doting entourage. Neither of us said a word on the way home, but when we got to the front door Jessie kissed me softly on the cheek.

Some things are better left unsaid — and no one says them better than Jessie.

CHAPTER 20

I PICKED up the telephone receiver. My head was still throbbing with the after-effects of doing battle with Steve. The tenderness in my ribs prevented me from doing anything more strenuous than impersonating a corpse. I spoke in a near whisper.

"Hello."

"Hi, Lenny. It's Rebecca."

Rebecca? It didn't seem possible that she could have already heard about my fight with Steve, but it did seem strangely coincidental that she should call only moments after I got back to the house. Since I didn't want to ask her outright if she knew about it, I figured I would play it casual.

"Oh, hi. How are you doing?"

"Okay, thanks. How about you?"

That brief conversational exchange was all I needed to assure myself that Rebecca did *not* know about the fight. Her voice was calm and level without a trace of tension. So since she wasn't calling to inquire about my battle scars, why was she calling? Our relationship had cooled a bit over the preceding week as I had done my best to avoid bumping into her at lunch or in the halls. It wasn't that my feelings about her had changed — not by any means. I simply had decided to devote my full attention to helping Jessie with the *Tarmac*. And to a certain extent, I held it against Rebecca for lending her talents to help make the *Landing Strip* a success. Now that I heard her voice on the phone, however, I cursed myself for being so stupid as to purposely ignore the most fascinating girl I had ever met. Sometimes I'm astoundingly dumb.

"So, Rebecca," I said, trying to sound cavalier, worldly, and as cool as the proverbial cucumber, "what's new with the prettiest girl this side of the Mississippi?"

"Save the flattery for someone else, Lenny, and tell me why you've been avoiding me. There's something wrong, and I want to know what it is. This just isn't like you."

It's hard to believe that a girl with all the captivating charm and beauty of Rebecca could also be so damn smart. Not that she'd have to be an Einstein to notice that I was purposely going out of my way to avoid seeing her, but from the tone of her voice it was clear that she had no doubts as to the reason behind my cold shoulder campaign. Most girls would figure that the problem was with them and that I had simply lost interest. That line of reasoning would never occur to Rebecca. She knew that she had landed me hook, line, and sinker, and it was inconceivable to her that I might have lost interest. Arrogance is not a trait I particularly admire, but Rebecca's sense of self-confidence was not at all intimidating and was, in fact, rather becoming.

"I've been kind of busy lately, Rebecca. I'm sorry if it seemed like I was ignoring you."

"That's a lot of garbage and you know it. You're mad at me, and instead of talking to me about it, you run away and hide like a little kid."

Rebecca could be a real tough cookie. She sounded

like a female reincarnation of Perry Mason. She was determined to cross-examine me until I admitted my guilt and pleaded for forgiveness. There was no way I could win. All I could hope for was to get it over with as quickly and painlessly as possible.

"Okay, you're right. I was a jerk from the word go. But you shouldn't hold that against me. After all," I said with a chuckle designed to charm away Rebecca's anger, "it takes a big man to admit he was wrong. And it takes an even bigger man to admit he was stupid. I confess to both counts." Rebecca let out a little giggle that I immediately interpreted as a sign of encouragement. "And since I'm still my same old cute and adorable self, and since I still think you're pretty enough to be one of Charlie's Angels, and since I still like you more than baseball, skateboarding, or potato chips, it just wouldn't make sense to let a little thing like my stupidity interfere with the great thing we have going."

"You really are a jerk, Lenny. But I guess I must be one, too, because I accept your apology and hereby extend a gracious invitation to you to join me for dinner. Mom and Dad are going out to a restaurant so we'll have the house all to ourselves. I'll cook you a meal like you've never eaten before."

Needless to say, an evening alone with Rebecca was the kind of dream that kept me awake at night, but I didn't want her to see me in my battered condition.

"It sounds great, but I really don't think I can."

"Oh, come on. Are you afraid I might try to take advantage of you?" she teased.

"Well, I do realize I'm rather irresistible, but that's not why. I'm just not feeling so good right now."

As soon as I said it, I knew it was the poorest excuse I

could have possibly come up with. Now she was certainly going to ask what the problem was.

"What's the matter?" she asked.

(Didn't I tell you?)

"Nothing really," I sputtered, fumbling for words. "Let's just say I had a hard day."

"Well, maybe what you need is to get out and relax a little. Come on, Lenny. It'll be fun."

"I really can't," I said.

It was becoming increasingly obvious that Rebecca was not going to take no for an answer. I was not in the mood to argue, so I figured I might as well level with her.

"The truth of the matter," I said, "is that I was in a fight this afternoon and I'm still a little sore."

"You were in a fight! Oh, my God! What happened?"

"It shouldn't be too hard to figure out. There's only one guy in the whole school that I can't stand the sight of, and I was lucky enough to experience the pleasure of shoving my fist down his throat."

"Steve? . . . You and Steve? . . . I can't believe it. What started it?"

"His big mouth started it, what else? He was gloating about the *Landing Strip* and then asked me and Jessie to sign his stupid petition."

"What petition?" she asked.

"He wants to get his paper recognized as the official school newspaper. Don't you know about it?"

"No. Not really. I mean he mentioned that possibility at the last meeting, but I thought he was just shooting off his mouth. I never believed he was serious."

"Well, he's very serious," I said. "And he's very crazy, and he's very sneaky, and I wouldn't put anything past him. But I'll be damned if I'm going to let him win."

The telephone line went silent for a few moments. I shifted the receiver to my other ear and waited for Rebecca to respond.

"I've got to agree with you, Lenny. He's gone too far this time. He's really flipping out."

I nodded my head but realized that she couldn't see me and answered with a mumbled "Yeah."

"Tell Jessie I'm sorry about the way things are turning out. And tell her I'd be more than willing to help out with the *Tarmac*. I hate to see her get hurt like this."

"That's sweet of you, Rebecca. You keep amazing me with how nice you really are."

"Don't be a sappy jerk, Lenny. Just tell me you're coming over for dinner, hang up the phone, and get your cute little body over here."

Now I ask you: In all sincerity, how could I possibly turn down an invitation like that? Obviously I couldn't. So I didn't.

And I'm glad I didn't.

CHAPTER 21

IT TOOK Steve only a couple of hours to get the required number of signatures on his petition. The Student Council had a meeting scheduled for the following afternoon, at which Steve displayed his usual flair for the dramatic. He was dressed to kill in a dark blue, three-piece corduroy suit, a deep yellow tailored shirt with gold cufflinks, and a tightly knotted silk tie. He looked like an underage district attorney about to plead his first case before the Supreme Court. He took a seat near the front of the room and waited for the Council members to finish their preliminary business.

Jessie, Rick, and I were sitting a little farther back in the room and we observed Steve's entrance with a mixture of concern and wonderment. The reasons for our concern were obvious. We were entering the final rounds of our world championship fight with Steve and the *Landing Strip,* and at that point the match would have to have been scored a draw. Steve was gearing up for one giant knockout punch and we were in the position of being on the defensive. Unfortunately, as every sports fan knows, the offensive team scores a lot more points than the defensive, so we were justifiably worried. Our sense of wonder, on the other hand, was a result of the mindboggling mess that Steve had stirred up. The school year that had begun with so much promise was now threatening to explode in our faces, and all through the efforts of one crazy kid who let his inflated ego get in the way of common sense. Crazy as he is, though, Steve was determined to fight it out to the bitter end. We were amazed by his incredible capacity for selfishness, self-righteousness, and contempt for anybody with a different opinion. The psychology departments at Harvard or Yale ought to do a detailed study of Steve. Maybe a chemical imbalance or poor toilet training fouled up his early development.

Steve glanced back at us as the Council members were voting acceptance of the secretary's report of the previous meeting. He smiled and gave us the "okay" sign with his thumb and forefinger. To this day I'm not at all sure what he was trying to say, but I answered him with a hand signal of my own. And there was no mistaking what *I* was trying to say.

After a couple of boring committee reports and a brief discussion of the school dress code, Patrice McNeill, the Student Council president, opened the meeting to questions from the floor. Steve's arm immediately shot up into the air waving frantically for recognition. The speed of his response was so immediate and so exaggerated that it drew laughter from almost everyone present. Steve was momentarily embarrassed, but he forced himself to chuckle loudly, trying to convince us that we were laughing with him and not at him.

He waited for absolute quiet and then read his petition, speaking very slowly and precisely. He enunciated each "Whereas" with all the assurance of a seasoned trial lawyer.

"Would you like me to read aloud the signatures we've

collected? I've got about a hundred and thirty of them," he boasted, "even though we only needed seventy-five."

"That won't be necessary," said Patrice. "We'll go over the signatures later, and if everything seems to be in order, it will be put on the ballot for the student elections."

"Thank you very much, Patrice," said Steve grandly. "I'm quite sure it will all check out perfectly."

"We'll be the ones to decide that, Steve," said Patrice. I could tell she was a little annoyed with Steve's pompous manner and she was trying hard to remain patient and polite. "Is that all?"

Steve nodded assent and sat down. There were no other motions from the floor so Patrice adjourned the meeting. I had expected Steve to come over to us and rub some salt into our wounds, but he exited quickly through a side door. By the time we got to the hall, he had disappeared.

"He's probably too ashamed to meet us face to face," said Rick.

"That's not very likely considering all the other things he's done that he's not ashamed of," said Jessie.

"Maybe he's just afraid that I'd beat the crap out of him again," I said. I was holding my fists out in front of me and shadow boxing like the great Muhammed Ali.

Rick laughed and Jessie put her arm around my waist, giving me a little hug.

"Maybe," she said, "but if I were Steve, I'd be in the best mood of my life and I wouldn't want to ruin it by hanging around with three spoilsports like us."

"That's true," said Rick. "But on the other hand, if I were Steve, I wouldn't want to ruin anybody else's good mood by *ever* hanging around with them."

"And if I were Steve," I said, "I wouldn't even want to

hang around with myself, so I'd probably feel compelled to flush myself down the toilet."

The three of us joked about that image for quite a while. By the time we had exhausted every possible variation of the theme, we had walked halfway home and were in surprisingly good spirits. Jessie's face was beaming brightly, as though she didn't have a care in the world. Rick was walking with a lively bounce to his step that was infectious with its enthusiasm. And I was laughing so hard that my sides ached and my cheeks felt numb.

Steve is a constant pain in the old derriere, but he is also an eternal source of merriment, so there are times when I kind of like having him around. Of course, I would like to be able to keep him locked up and let him out only when I need to laugh, but then you can't have everything.

CHAPTER 22

THERE'S nothing like Saturday night and a date with a beautiful girl to take your mind off your troubles.

Rebecca and I were sitting in the back seat of Rick's father's Pontiac. My arm was wrapped tightly around her shoulders and the scent of her freshly washed hair was sending chills up and down my spine. Jessie was sitting in the middle of the front seat primping herself in the rearview mirror. We were parked across the street from Academy Liquors, where Rick was doing his best to look, act, and sound like he was old enough to buy some liquid refreshments. He had his older brother's ID to fall back on if the clerk asked for proof of age, but even that didn't always work. Sometimes you'd have to stand outside and ask people going in if they would buy for you. I could never get up the nerve to do it, but Rick liked beer enough to use that technique on many occasions. Anyway, when we saw Rick bopping out of the store with a swagger and a big smile (and the unmistakable brown paper bag), we knew immediately that no further effort was necessary. We had it "made in the shade," as my dopey cousin likes to say.

"No problem?" asked Jessie.

"Come on," said Rick drawing out each word mockingly and doing a pretty good impersonation of Humphrey Bogart. "Have I ever disappointed you, baby?"

"Not that I can talk about in mixed company," said Jessie, coming back with a perfect retort à la Mae West.

"Would you two clowns cut the dramatics and get this buggy on the road?" said Rebecca. "The movie starts in fifteen minutes."

"Yeah, and I'm getting awfully thirsty," I added.

Rick twisted open a bottle of Schaefer and handed it back to me.

"Here you go, buddy," he said. "This ought to hold you for a while. Anybody else want one?"

Both girls nodded and Rick opened two more bottles. He took a swig of Jessie's and then started the engine. He slowly moved away from the curb and drove with all the attentiveness of someone taking an examination for a driver's license. The last thing he wanted was to be pulled over by a policeman, so he made sure to obey every sign right down to the letter. He was being so careful that it was making me nervous. But I guess it was better for me to be nervous than him.

The drive-in was featuring a horror twin-bill: *Disco Nightmare,* a low budget flick that detailed the adventures of a handsome vampire who liked to dance almost as much as he liked to draw blood, and *The She-Monster,* another vampire yarn in which a mysterious virus turns all fifty contestants in the Miss America pageant into a crazed army of seductive monsters. Neither of the movies was ever going to win any kind of an award, but it didn't much matter to any of us. Nobody, after all, goes to a drive-in to watch the movie. There are lots of better things to do.

Happily, Rebecca agreed with that idea so we made

ourselves very comfortable, kissing and cuddling and keeping each other nice and warm. I noticed that Jessie and Rick were also losing little time in getting to know each other better.

As I write this, I realize there were a few curious thoughts going through my mind back then. I mean, there I was fooling around with Rebecca, and I was worrying about my sister, wanting to make sure that she didn't let Rick go too far. Even I realize how contradictory that sounds, but in my heart of hearts that's exactly how I felt. It did have its beneficial effects, however, because I forced myself to set a good example for Rick by not moving my hands to places where Rebecca didn't want them. Of course, Rick probably never even noticed, but Rebecca certainly did.

"Thanks, Lenny," she said as we walked to the snack bar after the first movie. She was clutching my arm tightly and her voice was so loving that it almost frightened me.

"Thanks for what?" I asked.

"You know. For being so nice. For not trying to pressure me." She squeezed my arm even tighter. I was amazed at the strength in her grip. I figured I'd probably have a big black-and-blue mark in the morning, but I didn't dare pull my arm away. "It's just not the right time. Someday maybe, but not yet."

Now in all honesty, the anticipation of that "someday" excited me to the point where I almost bit off my tongue and wet my pants simultaneously. Luckily, I did neither. Rather, I squeezed Rebecca just as hard as she was squeezing me. I assured her that I cared about her and didn't care if all we ever did was shake hands — just as long as we could be together. I sounded so sincere that I almost convinced myself, but the image of that glorious "someday" kept flashing through my mind and I could hardly wait to experience it. I knew it would be fantastic.

The snack bar was incredibly crowded, but Rebecca knew one of the kids working behind the counter so we managed to place our order without having to wait in line. I was experiencing my usual craving for junk food and ordered a bucket of hot, buttered popcorn and a large Coke. Rebecca had a cheeseburger and vanilla shake, and we brought back some hot dogs for Jessie and Rick.

As we were walking back to the car, we came across Lorraine getting out of the back seat of Steve's car. She was hurriedly tucking in her blouse and she giggled when she saw us. Steve followed her out of the car and greeted us with a big smirk.

"Isn't it a little late for you kids to be out?" he said.

"Don't start in with me, Steve," I warned. "I've had just about all I'm gonna take from you."

"That's pretty big talk from such a little guy," he said.

I started to move toward him, planning to decorate his face with my fist, but Rebecca grabbed my arm and held me back.

"And you, Rebecca," he continued. "I just don't understand it. Why are you wasting your time with a jerk like this? I'm actually surprised that he even goes out with girls."

Steve's voice took on an exaggerated lisp. He waved a limp wrist at us as Lorraine led him away to the snack bar. If Rebecca hadn't been with me, I would've gone right after him and pounded him over the head until he admitted that he was the lowest form of life known to man.

"I could have killed him," I repeated to Rick when we got back in the car, "and loved every single minute of it."

"He really is a creep," agreed Rebecca.

"There's got to be something we can do to get even with him," said Jessie. I could tell she'd been drinking because she would never make a suggestion like that if she'd been totally sober.

"Why don't we let the air out of his tires?" suggested Rebecca.

Rick and I shook our heads in unison.

"Not imaginative enough," I said.

"That's right, we need something really special for sweet little Steven," said Rick. "Maybe I've got just the thing." He reached into the glove compartment and took out a small toolcase. He opened it and removed a small tube. He muttered a barely audible "Perfect" and motioned for me to follow him.

"What is it?" I asked as we walked towards Steve's car.

"It's Wonder Glue. It'll fix anything." He let out a very short and very devilish laugh. "And it's sure going to fix Steve's wagon."

I still wasn't quite sure what he had in mind but I followed along anyway.

Steve and Lorraine had not yet returned from the refreshment stand. Rick asked me to stand guard while he worked. He lifted the drive-in speaker from its resting place on the driver's window and dabbed two or three drops of the glue along the edge. He then set it back on the window and held it in place for a few moments.

"All done," he said. "He'll need a sledge hammer to get that off."

We hurried back to Rick's car and told the girls what we had done.

"Don't you think that seems a little cruel?" Jessie asked.

"What do you mean, cruel?" said Rick. "You're the one who wanted to get even with him."

"Yeah, but I thought you'd do something funny. I think maybe you've gone a little too far," she said.

"What if he tells the police?" asked Rebecca.

"Relax," I said, although that was a frightening possibility that had never occurred to me. "He doesn't know who did it."

"But don't you think he'll suspect? He's not that stupid," said Rebecca.

"So what," said Rick. "He doesn't have any proof so he can suspect all he wants."

"Well, I for one am worried," said Jessie.

Rick brushed away her worries with a wave of his hand and placed his arm around her shoulders. The second movie was about to start and we all relaxed, settling back into the positions we had been enjoying before the intermission.

I'm pleased to report that I saw even less of the second movie than I did of the first.

CHAPTER 23

Monday morning at school *everybody* was talking about the prank that had been pulled on Steve. Since the four of us had not stayed around the drive-in long enough to witness the results, most of what I heard was news to me. And all of it was music to my ears.

Evidently, Steve and Lorraine had gotten a little carried away with their kissing and hugging and didn't notice that the movies had ended or that everyone else had left. A security guard had to come over and knock on the window to hurry them along. Steve apologized in his most gentlemanly manner and tried to remove the speaker from his window. It refused to budge and Steve smiled weakly at the guard. "It's stuck," he said. The guard now figured he was dealing with a real smartass. He told Steve he had better get it unstuck real quick or be prepared to get it stuck somewhere else. Steve tried again but the speaker wouldn't give an inch. He repeated that it was stuck and told the guard to try for himself. As you can well imagine, the guard was not at all pleased to learn that the speaker had no intention of releasing its hold on the car window. Another guard came over to help, and then the manager appeared, but the best they could do was to dismantle the speaker so that only the plastic shell was attached to the window. That's the way Steve drove home, and that's pretty much how he drove to school on Monday. He had managed to chip away a lot of it, but there were enough traces of the battleship-gray plastic to remind him of that night for a long time to come. I was also pleased to learn that it was commonly accepted that Rick and I were responsible for the prank. No one had proof, of course, but it was nice to get credit for the deed.

My path didn't cross Steve's until the end of lunch period. I was eating with a group of friends and we were trading exaggerated details of our respective weekends. Steve interrupted us with his usual aplomb.

"Your ass is grass, Simpson," he said with a raspy slur that was meant to be overheard.

He walked away without waiting for a reply, which was fine with me because inane remarks like that don't really deserve a reply. Stupid people like Steve use them when they can't think of anything intelligent or original to say. It passes for witticism with some kids, but in my book it indicates a mental capacity that would be more appropriate for an amoeba. Nonetheless, Steve thought he had simultaneously scared the crap out of me and qualified himself for the Nobel Prize in Witticism. He walked away with a confident swagger and a satisfied smile.

"I don't understand why you act like you're surprised," said Rick later that afternoon. "Steve is by far the biggest jerk I've ever met and he outdoes himself with every new routine."

We were sitting in the *Tarmac* office. Rick was drinking a Pepsi and making a few minor corrections on some editorial copy. I wasn't doing much of anything. A lot of times when I don't feel like doing anything, I try to make it look like I'm doing something. This time I figured it really didn't make any difference. Rick didn't care and no one else was around — so why waste the energy pretending? I was content to sit back and devise diabolical schemes to terminate Steve's life and dispose of his body. I dismissed a few plans for being too obvious and a few others for being too intricate; but to this day, I honestly believe I came up with a couple of solid, foolproof schemes. Needless to say, I never would have put one of my plans into action, but I got a lot of joy from just thinking about them.

After about ten minutes of silence, Rick looked over at me and pursed his lips with a wry smile.

"You know," he said, "if Steve were a book or a movie, he'd be censored from coast to coast for having absolutely no socially redeeming value. He's repulsive from start to finish."

I laughed at the remark — not because it was so funny, but because Rick had obviously spent the last ten or fifteen minutes doing the same thing I was: counting all the ways that Steve was a creep. Somehow it was a very pleasurable activity.

Jessie walked into the room a short while later and I could tell immediately that something was wrong. Her face was flushed and her arms were folded tightly in front of her chest. I saw that she was about to cry and hurried over to her. I put my hands on her shoulders and without saying a word let her know it was okay to let everything out — I would understand and I would protect her. She threw her arms around me and started to cry with the heaving sobs of heartfelt pain.

"We're gonna lose it," she said with tears flowing down her cheeks. "We're gonna lose it all."

She pressed her face against my shoulder and lost

herself in two-months' worth of held-back tears and tensions. I didn't try to console her with meaningless platitudes because I wouldn't have believed them myself. What she needed most right then was the assurance that she was still loved and appreciated, and no one could have done that better than me. Somehow she needed a loving brother more than a boyfriend, so she was crying into my shoulder rather than Rick's. And though Rick was standing right beside us, he had the good sense not to intrude. She would need his assurance later, but right then she needed me.

Jessie and I go back a long way together. I mean, aside from the fact that we were born only a few minutes apart, we've been through a lot together. And as much as we argue and fight, there are still certain shared memories that bind us together in a very strong and very special way.

I remember when we were about seven years old and Grandma Simpson was in the hospital. She had suffered a heart attack, and though no one would tell us so, both Jessie and I knew she was going to die. She was in the intensive care ward, and it was hospital policy that children were not allowed to visit patients in that area. I guess they figured it was too depressing for young kids. They're probably right, but when the patient is someone you love as much as we loved our grandmother, you can put up with a lot more than that in return for a brief visit — especially when you're probably never going to see the person again. Jessie and I tried to get Dad to understand just how important it was for us to see Grandma again — even if only to say goodbye. The next day he sneaked us past the nurse's desk into Grandma's room.

I'll never forget her expression when she saw us walk into the room. She smiled and laughed and cried the most joyful tears I've ever seen. Jessie and I reacted in pretty much the same way. Dad left the room for a few minutes so we could be alone together and I noticed a few tears in his eyes, too, as he walked out the door. Jessie stood on one side of the bed and I stood on the other. We held Grandma's hands and talked about trivial things, but the words were nowhere as important as the feelings we were expressing.

When the nurse finally discovered us and asked us to leave, it was okay because we had shared a once-in-a-lifetime experience of total love and caring. Dad took us downstairs to the waiting room and then went back upstairs to spend some more time with Grandma. As soon as he left us, I fell into Jessie's arms and sobbed uncontrollably. She was the only one who could comfort me, and she did then just as I was comforting her now. When Grandma died two days later we cried again, but the tears were not as anguished as they would have been if we had not been able to say goodbye and tell her again how much we loved her.

So Jessie cried and cried into my shoulder. I held her tightly and stroked her hair, letting the storm run its course.

At my ripe old age, I suddenly came to the realization that life was an endless series of painful episodes, and the most you could hope for is to be present when someone you love needs comforting and to have that person present when you need comforting. People need people much more than they need money or nice clothes or flashy cars or student newspapers. The trouble is that everybody always forgets that.

CHAPTER 24

JESSIE cried for a long time. When she stopped she kissed me lightly on the cheek and dabbed at her eyes with a handkerchief. She smiled at Rick and squeezed his hand for a brief moment. She said she would be right back and went to the ladies' room to freshen up.

"I know I'm overreacting," she said when she got back, "but it's all beginning to hit home."

A few more tears began to well up in her eyes but she took a deep breath and forced them to recede.

"I was just talking to Patrice. She said the Student Council has okayed Steve's petition, so it's definitely going to be on the ballot. She was very apologetic about it. She seems to dislike Steve as much as we do, but he was extra careful with the petition and there wasn't a thing they could find to justify turning it down."

"So what's the big deal?" asked Rick. "Steve is careful about everything he does, so you should have assumed that he would never submit a petition that wasn't all fine and legal."

"The big deal," she said "is that we're probably going

to lose the election. That's what the big deal is, you big jerk."

"Don't you think it's a little early to concede defeat?" I asked.

"Not from what Patrice tells me. She and some of the other Council members have been doing some informal polling, and right now the *Tarmac* is losing. It's real close, but if the election were held today, in all likelihood we'd lose."

"It doesn't seem possible," said Rick. "How could anyone in his right mind vote for Steve over you?"

"First off, Rick," I said, "this is not a popularity contest between Steve and Jessie. That really shouldn't enter into it. People should be voting for or against the newspapers, not the editors."

"That's true," agreed Jessie, "but unfortunately that will work to Steve's advantage. Patrice felt that the only way we could be assured of winning was to turn it into a popularity contest — at least to a certain extent."

"That's a little unethical," said Rick, "but if it's our only option, I guess it's the route we'll have to take."

"Well, I think it stinks," I said. "If the only reason we win is because Jessie is prettier and funnier and more popular than Steve, then I'm not sure I want to win. I'm not sure I even want to play the game."

"It's our only chance, Lenny," argued Jessie. "I don't like it any more than you do, but if it's the only way, then we have to do it."

"No. *We* don't have to do it. Maybe you have to do it, and maybe Rick has to do it, but I don't want any part of it."

I grabbed my jacket and headed toward the door.

"It's our only chance, dammit!" shouted Jessie.

She started to cry again and threw herself into Rick's arms. I slammed the door and turned down the hall.

This time she needed Rick a lot more than she needed me. And I felt like I didn't need either of them.

CHAPTER 25

"Look, I have just as much right as anyone else to act like a crazy fool. That's the only explanation I can give for why I reacted like that."

"It really doesn't sound like you," said Rebecca.

"I know it doesn't sound like me, and I know I came across like a poster child for Idiot's Anonymous, but I did it anyway."

We were sitting in Rebecca's living room. I had gone there straight from the strange episode at the *Tarmac* office. My behavior had confused me, and I needed to talk to someone to try to figure out what had happened.

"I guess it was the combination of a whole bunch of things," I said. "Part of it was probably a defense mechanism. I was feeling just as angry and frustrated as Jessie, but I would have looked like a complete moron if I had started to cry like she did. That's one way girls have it easier than guys. They can cry anytime they want and no one thinks much about it. But if I had started to cry, the whole school would hear about it and I could never show my face again."

Rebecca nodded in agreement. I had half expected her to respond with some feminist arguments that men should be as free to express their emotions as women, but she didn't say a word.

"So, anyway, instead of crying I took out my anger on Jessie and Rick."

"I'm sure they'll understand if you explain it to them like that," said Rebecca.

"They probably will, but I've still got mixed feelings about it."

"You mean about the popularity contest?"

"Yeah. Mostly that. Part of it stems from the fact that Steve is so easy to hate that anybody short of Attila the Hun would be more popular. So if the *Tarmac* wins the election on that basis alone, it's not a vote of confidence or support at all. And if people honestly think the *Landing Strip* is a better newspaper, then it probably deserves to win. I don't know, Rebecca. I'm really mixed up."

"I don't think so," she said. "You sound pretty sensible to me. There are two sides to every issue, and you're just seeing both of them. There's nothing wrong with that."

"There is when nobody else agrees with you."

"First of all, Leonard Simpson, I agree with you. And it's not really true that Jessie disagrees with you. She's just too close to the situation to notice that there actually is another side."

Rebecca was smiling radiantly. She held my hand in her lap and lightly ran her fingers up and down my arm. And as if all that was not enough to distract my attention, here she was speaking with all the wisdom of a beloved and well-traveled great-grandmother. There were so many different aspects to Rebecca's personality — each of them more lovable than the other — that my mind reeled with the thought that I, out of all the guys at Fairfield, had won her heart. I couldn't be all bad if she still cared about me —

especially after hearing my ridiculous sob story. And if she didn't think I was a jerk, I probably wasn't.

The only problem was in convincing Jessie and Rick of that.

The immediate problem, however, was in figuring out how to change the subject to love, romance, kissing, hugging, and all the other delightful rewards of having a girl friend.

Happily, with Rebecca's generous cooperation it was no problem at all.

CHAPTER 26

"**Y**OU raised a good point, Lenny," said Rick. "But I think your approach could have been a little more tactful."

"Probably," I agreed. "But then again you weren't being the most open-minded person in the world, either."

"Well it's hard to be open-minded when someone's talking to you like you're an idiot."

"Did it ever occur to you that maybe you really are an idiot?"

"No," he said, "it didn't."

My question was offered with a smile and Rick's response was accompanied by a chuckle. Neither of us wanted to rehash our earlier disagreement, so we let the conversation slip into harmless teasing.

Rick had been sprawled across the couch in the downstairs family room when I arrived home from Rebecca's house. Jessie was upstairs washing up and changing her clothes. The television was on and my attention was captured by an ancient rerun of the original Superman series. It was a typical plot, with the mild-mannered Clark Kent acting his usual mild-mannered self, Lois Lane making goo-

107

goo eyes at Superman, and Jimmy, the irrepressible cub reporter, muttering "Gee whiz's" and "Holy Cow's" as he stumbled over his own feet and generally made a fool of himself. It was great!

At first it seemed kind of stupid to me that Clark Kent never told anyone that he was Superman, but then I figured it was pretty smart. I mean, obviously, Clark could have used his Superman abilities to good advantage. He could have been the greatest centerfielder and home run hitter the Yankees ever had, or he could have won a gold medal in every event at the Olympics. He could have gotten a big contract to advertise breakfast cereals, and he could have appeared on every television and radio talk show from coast to coast. But it would have got boring soon. And if Superman was around all the time and everybody knew who he was and where he could be reached, it would be one big, continuous hassle. Every punk muscleman from every two-bit hick town would swagger into Metropolis to see if they could beat Superman at weight lifting, arm wrestling or whatever. He'd never have any peace. And since no one could ever come close to matching Superman's strength, pretty soon people would start seeing him as a freak and a big, bad bully who picks on poor, unsuspecting strangers. It wouldn't be a very enjoyable life at all. So the more I thought about it, the more I figured Clark was being real smart not to tell anyone who he was. It made his life a lot simpler, and it kept a shroud of mystery around Superman so he could continue to fight for truth, justice, and the American way. What a guy!

Just as the episode was reaching its climax (Lois Lane being handcuffed and held for ransom by a ruthless madman), Jessie walked down the stairs. She stopped on the bottom step and greeted me with a hesitant "Hello."

108

"Don't look so dramatic," I said, "because I forgive you for everything."

"*You* forgive *me?*" she asked. "I'm the one who should be forgiving you."

"So what are you waiting for? I'm all ears."

"Okay, I forgive you," she said. "Or at least half of me forgives you. The other half thinks you might be smarter than you look and maybe I should listen to what you have to say."

"I've got to be smarter than I look, and sometimes I'm so smart it even surprises me. On the other hand," I added, "sometimes I'm so dumb that I make people forget how smart I actually am."

"Well you weren't being so dumb this afternoon. You made a lot of sense. Rick and I talked about it after you left and I think we're going to have to change our original strategy."

"Specifically?" I asked.

"Basically we have to convince everybody that the *Tarmac* is a more valuable student newspaper. Patrice said that both Steve and I will have an opportunity to present our arguments at the "Meet the Candidates" assembly next week. And I can't very well stand up on stage and ask people to vote for the *Tarmac* because I'm a nicer person than Steve. It just wouldn't go over."

"And besides," said Rick, "Mr. Polansky would never allow it."

"Yeah," said Jessie a little sheepishly. "Mr. Polansky stopped by the office after you left and urged us . . ."

"Urged us nothing," said Rick. "He *ordered* us."

"That's true," agreed Jessie. "He ordered us to run a clean and honest campaign. If we can't win honestly, he said, he'd rather not win at all."

"Gee," I said with a grin two-miles wide, "I think I hear an echo."

"Yeah, yeah, yeah," said Jessie. "Anyway, we've got to do it your way. Which means, of course, that if we lose, we have no one to blame but you."

Isn't that the way it always is? Damned if you do and damned if you don't. If you're dumb, that's its own punishment. If you're smart, your only reward is having everybody wait around hoping to catch you in a slip-up so they can prove that you really are as dumb as they thought in the first place.

Sometimes I think we'd all be better off following Clark Kent's example and not let anyone else know how smart we actually are. Few of us, though, are quite that smart.

CHAPTER 27

NEXT to Steve, the most despicable person in the school is Pete Alonzo. Pete looks like a cross between Neanderthal man and a frostfree refrigerator — with mental faculties to match. Pete has difficulty with even the most elementary human tasks. I've never seen him eat without dribbling food all over himself, and I've never seen him walk more than ten paces without tripping over his own feet. He likes to liven up his conversation (and there's no question that it needs to be livened up) with four-letter words, and he thinks it's a lot of fun to belch and fart in public places. He also figures there's no sense carrying a handkerchief when his shirtsleeve is so handy. Everything about Pete is laughable, but it's rare that anyone ever laughs at him. The fact that he has the combined strength of two mules probably accounts for this, but he also happens to be the son of the Chief of Police. In a small town that kind of prestige goes a long way.

With credentials like these, it shouldn't come as a surprise that Pete is among Steve's closest friends. He was also the one chosen to personally deliver a handwritten note from Steve the next day at school. The message was concise: "I'll be in the *Landing Strip* office at 3:00. Please come see me. It's important."

I received the note during my third period American history class and was unable to concentrate for the rest of the day. I didn't mention the message to anyone — not even Jessie. I didn't want to be talked out of going to meet Steve, nor did I want to be talked into it. I was unsure how to handle the situation from the moment it fell into my lap. My first impulse was to return the note to Steve with instructions to forthrightly shove it, but my curiosity was aroused and I wanted to hear whatever it was Steve had to say.

It was a mistake.

Steve was the only one in the office when I arrived. He was sitting behind a desk and motioned for me to sit down. He looked genuinely pleased to see me. I knew that was a bad omen.

"You know, Lenny," he said, "in spite of our differences in the past, I've always liked you. That's why I asked you to come talk to me today. It disturbs me to see you be made a fool of, and I'd like to help put a stop to it."

Here we go again, I thought, another pretentious lecture on why the *Landing Strip* is a better paper than the *Tarmac* and why don't I see the light and come over to the winning side.

"Forget it, Steve," I said. "I've heard all of this before and I . . ."

"No, Lenny. You haven't heard this part before."

The expression on Steve's face changed completely. His smile became diabolical and he spoke with an eerie tone that was bone-chilling.

"I feel compelled to tell you that your sweet little girl friend, Rebecca, is not quite as sweet as she seems. In fact, she's something of a two-timer."

"You're full of crap and you know it." I could feel my face flush a bright crimson. My fist was clenched, getting ready to smash itself against Steve's jaw.

"Well, she's not really two-timing you in the usual sense. I mean she's not going out with other guys. Not that I know of, at least. But she's still using you and making you look like a fool."

I jumped from my chair and grabbed Steve by the collar. I pushed him down to the floor and poised my fist inches away from his lying mouth.

He started laughing. He started to laugh as hard as I had ever seen anyone laugh before. And in between his fits of laughter he kept repeating the same phrase: "She's been spying on you. She's a spy."

I released his collar from my grip. I slumped back and leaned against the side of the desk. He had to be lying. He had to be.

"I can prove it, of course," he said finally, with one last burst of laughter. "She's been reporting back to me about all of your *Tarmac* meetings right from the start. For example, she told me all about the argument you had with Jessie and Rick yesterday. And, by the way, I do want to thank you for being such an honorable character. You're really not a bad guy."

"I don't know how you heard about it," I said, "but I'm sure it wasn't from Rebecca. You're lying. I don't know what you're trying to accomplish, but I know you're lying."

"Think about it some more, Lenny. You, Jessie, and Rick were the only people there — so do you really think Jessie or Rick told me about it? You're not that dumb."

I got up from the floor glaring at Steve with all the hate my reeling heart and mind could muster. I headed for the door.

"Anyway," said Steve with a spiteful chuckle, "I just wanted you to know the facts before you went out and bought her an expensive Christmas present."

"I can't stand the sight of you," I said. "You're as low and as stinking as they come, and I don't believe you've ever told the truth in your life. And I don't believe a word you're saying now."

I slammed the door behind me and stomped down the hall.

The trouble was that I did believe him.

CHAPTER 28

ON MY way to Rebecca's house, I was determined that I would remain cool, calm, and collected. I would be a picture of tranquility: sensible, rational, and openminded. I would listen to whatever explanation Rebecca offered and I would not jump to hasty conclusions. I was determined to be as patient and logical as an old Hindu monk. The problem with all that was that I was a young American adolescent male with a strong case of the hots for a lovely young adolescent female who seemed to be doing me wrong.

For some reason, I believed Steve without reservation — I had as soon as he had said it.

He had to find out about my argument with Jessie and Rick from someone, and I knew it couldn't have been from one of them. No one else had been around (with the exception, of course, of Mr. Polansky, who was the least likely stool pigeon of all), and neither Jessie nor Rick would have mentioned it to a soul. I had told only Rebecca. She had to be the one.

So when I knocked on Rebecca's front door I was firmly convinced of her guilt. I was equally convinced that she would deny my accusations for a while and would then fall tearfully into my arms confessing everything and begging to be forgiven.

When she opened the door, I hadn't yet decided whether or not to forgive her.

"Hi, Lenny," she said. "What a nice surprise. I was just thinking about you."

"Oh, really? Well, I guess that's better than having you talk about me."

My words came out sounding much harsher than I had intended and Rebecca reacted with a puzzled look.

"What's that supposed to mean?" she asked. "Is something wrong.?"

I shrugged my shoulders and pursed my lips in a grim-looking pout. Rebecca reached out her hand and touched my arm, but I did not allow myself to acknowledge the gesture. I was acting out some kind of a super-macho, tough-guy script from a B movie. What I didn't realize, however, was that I was playing the part of the bad guy.

I followed Rebecca into the living room and sat in an armchair opposite the couch. Now that probably doesn't sound like a big deal, but since I usually sat next to her on the couch so we could hold hands as we talked, it was a significant enough change that Rebecca immediately sensed its import.

"What's wrong with you?" she demanded. "Would you please tell me what's going on?"

"Why don't *you* tell *me* what's going on?" I said sarcastically.

"Don't play games with me, Lenny. You're beginning to make me very angry and I don't even know why."

"Don't act so put out," I said, "because you're no-where near as mad as I am."   .

"Are you ever going to tell me why you're so ticked off or are you going to keep talking in circles?"

I took a deep breath and then let everything out.

"I'm angry because I don't like being mistreated. I don't like being lied to and I don't like being made to look like a fool. And I'm especially angry because the person doing all of this is you." I paused and could feel my voice tremble with the weight of a thousand different emotions. "I trusted you, Rebecca. I really trusted you."

"And I haven't done anything to lose your trust," she said.

Rebecca got up from the couch and came over to me. She placed her arm around my shoulder and squeezed gently.

"Please tell me what's bothering you so we can talk about it," she said.

There was something about the way she said that and something about the way she touched my shoulder that made me lose all self-control. I stood up and started shouting at her, flailing my arms as I screamed accusations. I told her — or rather yelled at her — what I had learned from Steve. I told her she might just as well confess because I knew the whole story anyway. When she calmly denied it, I told her she was full of crap and was nothing but a cheap, two-timing, lying cheat. I called her every foul name I could think of and invented lots of new ones. By the time I was finished with my ranting and raving, my voice was hoarse, my face was lathered with beads of clammy perspiration, and I could hardly catch my breath. I stood in front of Rebecca limp and exhausted like the proverbial wet dishrag.

Rebecca looked at me blankly as a single tear slowly slid down her cheek. She hadn't said a word for the last two or three minutes of my tantrum, and she continued to study me silently for a few moments more. When she finally spoke, her voice was as distant and emotionless as the recorded message on a telephone answering service.

"Get out," was all she said.

I didn't even think about protesting.

CHAPTER 29

THERE was no question about it. I had blown it. My relationship with Rebecca would never and could never be the same. For all practical purposes our relationship was over, and I placed all the blame for that on me — not on Rebecca. I still believed she had been reporting back to Steve, but that no longer mattered. The only thing that mattered was that I had not allowed her the opportunity to explain. I had refused to let her speak and wouldn't listen to anything she had to say. She might have been the guilty party, but I was the fool.

Fool. That's the exact term Rick and Jessie would have used to describe me if they had known about Rebecca's spying activities. I would have had to listen to five-hundred "I-told-you-so's" and countless cruel and insulting remarks directed at Rebecca, the only girl I had ever loved and the girl I continued to adore despite everything that had happened. I was a fool when it came to her, but I was not going to let anyone know just how foolish I had been. So I never mentioned Rebecca's transgression or our ensuing argument to anyone. In addition to the fact that I didn't want to hear Rick's snide remarks and gloating satisfaction, I also didn't see what purpose would be served by spreading the news of Rebecca's actions. The harm had already been done, and no amount of cursing and swearing was going to turn the clock back. Rebecca had made a mistake and now we were both paying for it.

While I had resolved that I would not tell a soul about Rebecca's extracurricular activities, there was no way I could hide the fact that she and I had called it quits. My face told the whole story. As soon as I walked into the house after the scene at Rebecca's, Jessie rushed over to ask what was wrong. I could hardly talk at the time and mumbled something about seeing her later. I went to my room, plugged my headphones into the stereo, turned the volume a quarter turn higher than it had ever been before, and tried to lose myself in Mick Jagger and the Rolling Stones.

I discovered this technique a few years ago — its great for forgetting whatever happens to be troubling me. I find it practically impossible to think about anything while listening to hard rock that's turned up so loud it sounds like a Harley-Davidson is peeling out between my ears. It must have helped a little because a half hour later I was able to talk to Jessie about what had happened. And even though I was lying to her about the specific details of our breakup, it was still helpful. I told her that I had discovered that Rebecca was still seeing her old boyfriend on the sly, and when I confronted her with it we had a riproaring fight.

"Well it seems to me that you had a perfect right to get angry," said Jessie. "She was cheating on you."

"I know, but no matter how justified I was, it still hurts a lot," I said. "You know how crazy I was about her. Well I'm still crazy about her and I'm afraid I'm going to be for a long time. She was the best thing that ever happened to me, and it seems like I've thrown it all away for nothing."

"I wouldn't exactly call Rebecca's cheating nothing, so you're not the one who loused things up. She did."

"I know, I know," I said nodding my head sadly. But I didn't know and Jessie didn't know, and I simply wanted the discussion to end and I didn't want to talk about it anymore. Jessie is not the type to push a conversation beyond its limits, and she clearly sensed that I had no more to say. She smiled tenderly, and without saying a word assured me that if I ever needed to talk about it some more, she would be there.

The next few days were among the saddest in my life. I hardly spoke to anyone, and when I did speak, my voice had a doomsday tenor to it that depressed everyone within earshot. Needless to say, I was not the best company and no one stayed within earshot for long.

In spite of my gloominess, however, I tried to go along with my life as usual. I went to school, did my homework, listened to music and watched television. I even forced myself to attend a meeting of the *Tarmac* staff. That was particularly difficult because it was an added reminder of why Rebecca and I had split up, but I felt it was something I *should* do — if only to help get the hurt out of my system.

So I sat in the *Tarmac* office and daydreamed while Jessie, Rick, Eddie, Denise, and a few other kids planned strategy. Since the "Meet the Candidates" program was scheduled for the next day, this meeting was looked upon as the be-all and end-all of strategy sessions. It was now or never.

The program would be moderated by the Student Council, and Jessie and Steve would each be allowed to make a five-minute presentation in favor of their respective newspapers. From what I could gather (and I unashamedly admit that I was only half listening), Jessie was going to rely quite heavily on tradition in her defense of the *Tarmac*. ("It was the school newspaper of your grandparents and great-grandparents.") She would also argue that it was wrong to say that the paper had not changed over the years. It was, in fact, a very different paper from the one that existed twenty or thirty years ago. She illustrated the point with an excerpt from the November, 1947 issue of the paper, which described the goings-on at the annual homecoming dance. It was a hilarious example of the "Golly, gee, didn't we have fun" style of student journalism, and it made Jessie's point abundantly clear. Jessie's final argument was that working on a student newspaper should be a learning experience — both for the reporters and the reading audience — and the standard set by the *Tarmac* was a far better teacher than anything the *Landing Strip* could offer.

All in all I felt it would be a pretty effective presentation.

Too bad Jessie never got the chance to use it.

CHAPTER 30

THE meeting came to a close shortly after Jessie's practice run-through of her speech. Most of the kids praised her performance, wished her luck on the next day's program, and went on their way. Jessie, Rick, and I were the last to leave.

"What's the matter, Lenny?" asked Rick. "You seem a little out of it. Are you still pining for Rebecca?"

I didn't respond to Rick but simply glared at him with a what-are-you-some-kind-of-an-idiot expression.

"Don't be so understanding, Rick," said Jessie sarcastically. "It's only been a couple of days since they broke up. Can't you try and act like a normal human being once in a while?"

Rick shrugged his shoulders sheepishly and his face blushed with embarrassment.

"I'm sorry," he said. "I didn't mean it the way it sounded. I was just kidding around."

"Don't worry about it," I said casually. "It's okay."

The three of us gathered our belongings and walked toward the door. Jessie switched off the lights and Rick opened the door to the hallway. We each took one step into

123

the hall and halted in dumbfounded amazement. We were all looking at the same thing.

Mr. Renaldo and Steve were walking out of the next room. Actually, Mr. Renaldo was the one who was walking. Steve was being led like a naughty child. His arm was being gripped tightly by Mr. Renaldo, and although he was not struggling very forcefully, he was obviously none too pleased with his predicament. Mr. Renaldo was really fired up. His teeth were clenched and the muscles in his jaw were bulging. He looked like he was using all of his self-control to stop from beating the life out of Steve right then and there. He pulled Steve along with him down the hall and the two of them entered the office of Mr. Costello, the principal.

None of us had any idea what had just happened, but we all agreed that we were now playing in an entirely different ball game.

CHAPTER 31

As I'VE said earlier, news travels fast at Fairfield, and the rumors start flying way before the news is confirmed. Not surprisingly, then, our phone started ringing the minute we got home and didn't stop until close to 11:00. All of the conversation centered on what had happened between Mr. Renaldo and Steve, and all of it was hearsay — although a few kids claimed to have inside information from some "very reliable sources."

Guessing games are not my forte, so I pretty much stayed out of the "What do you think he did?" sweepstakes. I figured we'd learn soon enough, and if it was bad news, I'd rather put if off as long as possible. If it was good news, I wouldn't be able to enjoy it fully in my present state of mind anyway, so I couldn't see the point in worrying myself sick about it. Besides, I still had other things to worry about.

I didn't have to wait too long for an explanation. First thing the next morning at school, Mr. Polansky's voice came over the P.A. system and asked that the *Tarmac* staff meet with him at the end of homeroom period. Jessie and I glanced at each other as soon as the announcement was completed. We both knew that the meeting had to be about Steve. We were right.

Mr. Polansky's face was solemn as Jessie and I entered the *Tarmac* office. Mr. Renaldo was sitting beside him and they were talking quietly to each other. Mr. Polansky nodded his head slightly to acknowledge our arrival, but his face never lost its grave expression. Rick, Eddie, and Denise had arrived before us and were already seated in the second row of chairs. Rick offered a rather meek hello and Denise smiled halfheartedly. We all looked and felt like we were attending a funeral — only none of us knew who the corpse was going to be. Jessie and I sat down and waited for Mr. Polansky and Mr. Renaldo to get the show on the road. They talked privately for another two or three minutes and then turned their attention to the rest of us.

"Steven Braverman has been suspended," said Mr. Polansky.

Mr. Polansky paused to allow his words to penetrate and allow us time to catch our collective breath. Whatever Steve had done was no joking matter. Suspension is big-time stuff and it is not done lightly.

"He was involved in gross misconduct and he has to face the penalty," said Mr. Renaldo. "And while it is highly irregular for a faculty member to discuss the academic or disciplinary record of a student with other students, I think that the present circumstances are unusual enough to warrant some explanation. Expecially since you were the target and victims of Steve's wrongdoing."

I noticed for the first time the tape recorder that was sitting on the desk in front of Mr. Renaldo. He moved it a little closer to himself and fiddled with the controls. He looked at everyone in the room — individual by individual

126

— as though trying to prepare us for what we were about to hear. Then he clicked the recorder to the "on" position.

The voices that spoke sounded like they had been recorded inside a duffel bag. They were muffled, raspy, and a little garbled. They were also unmistakable.

Jessie was sitting right beside me and she reached over to place her hand on my arm. She squeezed me tightly and I could feel a slight tremble filter through her body. I glanced at her quickly, but I was unable to offer even a hint of a comforting smile. We all just sat there and listened silently like a bunch of catatonic zombies.

The recording had been made the previous day when we were in the *Tarmac* office discussing Jessie's strategy for the debate. How it had been made, and why it had been made were still questions that remained unanswered. There was no question, however, as to who was responsible.

The tape ended abruptly midway through Jessie's rehearsal of her closing comments. Mr. Renaldo switched off the machine and cleared his throat.

"I walked in at this point and discovered Steve. He had slipped a very sensitive wide-range microphone under the door that separated the two rooms. He couldn't hear what you were saying, but the recorder could pick it up," said Mr. Renaldo. "It was as big a shock to me then as it is to you now. It's inconceivable to me that he would have gone to such lengths to try to defeat you, but there's no disputing his guilt. He was caught with his hand deep inside the cookie jar."

"What effect does all of this have now?" asked Rick. "I mean what's going to happen with the election, with the *Landing Strip,* with all of us? This is just crazy."

"You're exactly right, Rick," said Mr. Polansky. "This

is crazy, and I don't think anyone is quite sure what all the ramifications will be. We are considering a few options, though."

"One thing that has been decided is the future of the *Landing Strip*," said Mr. Renaldo. "As far as I'm concerned it has no future. I'm resigning as its faculty advisor and I'm sure that no one will volunteer to replace me. Without faculty support, the newspaper will die a very quick death."

"What about the election?" I asked. "And the debate?"

"The election will go on as scheduled," said Mr. Renaldo. "The *Landing Strip* will be taken off the ballot so the *Tarmac* will be running unopposed. That's not really unusual. Even in the political world there are quite a few elections with only one candidate. As for the debate, I don't think it's necessary for Jessie to speak. It would be akin to kicking a dead horse, wouldn't you agree, Mr. Polansky?"

"Completely," he replied. "In fact, there isn't even a horse left to kick. For all practical purposes the *Landing Strip* is no more."

"Doesn't that seem a little unfair?" asked Jessie. "I mean, a lot of kids have worked hard on the paper, and it doesn't seem right to punish all of them because of Steve."

Everyone in the room, including the two teachers, stared at Jessie in disbelief. The collapse of the *Landing Strip* was exactly what she had been working toward for a couple of months; now, all of a sudden, she was feeling sorry for the losing team. I hate to sound like a typical male chauvinist pig, but sometimes I really can't figure girls out. One minute they're this and the next minute they're that. There's no rhyme or reason to them.

Mr. Polansky looked at Jessie for a few moments and gave her a fatherly smile.

"That's a very gracious and mature attitude, Jessie," he said. "And I'm proud of you for being able to look at the other side of the coin. Whenever there's a winner there also has to be a loser. Most of us, however, do not share your ability to show compassion to the losing side. It's a special gift, Jessie, and you should be proud of yourself."

I couldn't have agreed with him more. There was not an ounce of compassion in my soul at that particular moment. I was filled with outrage at the things Steve had done and the situation he had brought us to. I hated him with every muscle, fiber, membrane, and cell in my body. He had deliberately lied to me and tricked me into believing that Rebecca could not be trusted. I had broken off with the only girl I had ever cared about because I believed slimy Steve Braverman instead of her.

I was a fool and I probably deserved to lose her, but I wanted one more try to win her back.

CHAPTER 32

I HAD a hard time tracking down Rebecca that day, and I had an even harder time convincing her to meet me after school so we could talk things over.

"There's really nothing to talk about," she said. "You put on your big macho routine and got what you wanted. Your mind was made up right from the start so what's the point of talking?"

"I made a mistake, Rebecca, and I'm sorry. I really need to talk to you about it."

Rebecca's expression was so cold and unyielding that I took her hand in mine, trying to initiate some level of personal contact. She cringed at my touch and turned her eyes away from me.

"Please," I said.

Rebecca looked at me thoughtfully. She must have recognized the determination in my eyes because she finally nodded assent.

"I'll meet you by your locker at 3:00," I said.

She nodded again and hurried away from me. She wasn't going to make it easy for me, but at least she was going to give me another chance.

I met her after school and we headed for the Big Scoop, a local ice cream parlor. On the way we talked about the weather, how our classes were going — the usual stuff. Rebecca was obviously in no great hurry to talk about the subject at hand, and I was getting more nervous by the minute.

The Big Scoop was crowded as usual, but we managed to find a booth toward the back where we could talk with some degree of privacy. Rebecca ordered a hot fudge sundae and I had a banana-bonanza, the biggest item on the menu. I figured I would need all the sustenance I could get.

"I guess you've heard about Steve?" I said.

"No," she replied with uncharacteristic sarcasm. "I've been in Afghanistan all day. Of course I've heard about Steve. Hasn't everybody?"

"I guess so. But I don't think everybody knows that Steve was caught tape recording *Tarmac* staff meetings from the next room."

"You're kidding," she said. "That's unbelievable."

"Yeah, but it's also true. Evidently he's been doing it for a long time. That's how he tricked me into believing that you were spying on us and reporting back to him. He simply was repeating things he had heard with his eavesdropping equipment." I paused and sighed deeply. "I was stupid enough to believe him instead of you."

Rebecca nodded sadly.

"Yes," she said. "You were stupid, but what's past is past. Nobody reads yesterday's paper."

"So you forgive me?" I asked.

"Do I forgive you?" she repeated as though she didn't understand the question. "I suppose so. I mean I accept the fact that you were stupid and I accept the fact that you're sorry. If that means I forgive you, then I guess I do."

"Fantastic," I said. I felt an exuberance in my heart that had been missing for the last several days. I wanted to jump up and shout for joy.

"So what are you doing Saturday night?" I asked. "There's a couple of old science-fiction movies in town this week."

"I know," she said. "I've already made plans to see them."

"Well, can't your plans include me?" I said jokingly.

"I don't think that would go over too well with Roger," she said.

"Roger?"

My chin must have fallen about a foot and a half and I felt a grapefruit-sized lump appear mysteriously in my throat. Sometimes I don't believe how dense I can be. It never occurred to me that Rebecca would already have my replacement lined up. I was surprised and hurt.

"You don't believe in wasting any time, do you?" I asked.

Rebecca just looked at me silently. Her eyes were beginning to well up with tears. Her lower lip was quivering and she bit it in a futile attempt to calm herself. My own eyes were getting a little misty and I didn't want to make matters any worse than they were. If I was going to be antagonistic, I was not going to get anywhere.

"Well, maybe some other time," I suggested.

Rebecca studied me for a moment and shook her head slowly. I could see that she was straining to hold back the tears and trying to regain her composure.

I wasn't in any better shape. My face was flushed and my voice crackled whenever I spoke.

"Please, Rebecca, I need to see you again."

"No, Lenny," she said. "You made your choice when

you trusted Steve instead of me. All I ever asked of you was that you be honest with me and I would be honest with you. Evidently that was a little too much for you to handle. You were a stupid ass!"

Rebecca had lost the battle to stop herself from crying openly. The tears flowed like a hundred tiny rivers from her eyes. Her chest was heaving and she was having trouble catching her breath.

"You didn't trust me, Lenny. You wouldn't believe me."

I went around to her side of the booth and put my arms around her shoulders. I was trying to comfort her, but I only made it worse.

"Leave me alone," she said. "Just leave me alone!"

I went back to my side of the booth. There was nothing left to say. My relationship with Rebecca shared the fate of the *Landing Strip*.

It was over.

CHAPTER 33

THE election was anticlimactic. I mean there's something missing from the thrill of victory when you run unopposed. It's a little like being a benchwarmer on a championship baseball team: Your side may have won, but you didn't have very much to do with it and you're not sure if you even have the right to celebrate.

Nonetheless, winning is a lot better than losing, and congratulations came from everybody Jessie, Rick, and I had ever so much as spoken to. It was fun. We got a chance to be gracious and humble yet show just enough self-satisfaction to let people know we were feeling our oats and loving every minute of it.

Mr. Polansky called a meeting of the *Tarmac* staff for the afternoon following our election victory. We figured it would be a celebration party rather than a business meeting, but Mr. Polansky was all business as usual. He was accompanied by Mr. Renaldo, and after a few words of congratulations he got down to the nitty gritty of his presentation.

"The biggest danger we face now is becoming lack-adaisical and overconfident. The natural tendency will be to relax and take it easy, but that's the worst thing we can do.

Every successful journalist must strive to make his current work his best ever. Once he becomes content simply to duplicate the quality of his previous work he begins to fall backward. I don't want to see that happen to any of you or to the *Tarmac*."

There were some murmurs of approval from the staff, but most of us did not understand why we were being lectured at a time when we should have been dancing in the streets. I guess there's something about being a teacher that compels you to be stern no matter what the occasion.

"I have to agree with Mr. Polansky one hundred percent," said Mr. Renaldo. "There's always room for improvement, and despite Steve's excesses, that is really what the *Landing Strip* was all about. It was an attempt to improve upon the format and content of the *Tarmac*, and while it didn't always succeed, there were some things it did do better than the *Tarmac*."

We all grew silent at that remark, but it didn't bother Mr. Renaldo in the slightest and he continued with his train of thought.

"The truth of the matter," he said, "is that it would have been a very close election. The *Landing Strip* had a lot of student support."

"Yeah," said Jessie, "but it was all for the wrong reasons."

"That may be true," said Mr. Renaldo, "but whatever the reasons, the majority rules in an election. I think a majority vote could easily have gone to either side."

"There's no question about it," said Rick. "It would have been a very close election. But so what? I don't think I understand the point you're trying to make."

Mr. Renaldo studied Rick thoughtfully as though trying to decide whether or not to respond to him.

"I guess it's a point I don't want to belabor," he said. "But the reason there was an election in the first place was to respond to some student dissatisfaction with the *Tarmac*."

"Steve was the only one who . . ." interrupted Rick.

"Please let me finish, Rick," said Mr. Renaldo. "There were a number of students who saw a need for another kind of publication and they chose to fill that need with the *Landing Strip*. Their experiment proved to be quite successful. So successful, in fact, that it seems foolish and unnecessary to throw it all away."

Mr. Renaldo glanced over at Mr. Polansky and with a slight nod of his head offered him the floor.

"Mr. Renaldo and I have done quite a bit of talking since our last meeting," he said, " and we're in agreement on a number of key issues. First and foremost, we were both very impressed and heartened by Jessie's comment concerning the current status of the other *Landing Strip* staff members. She's right. It doesn't seem fair that they should be punished because of Steve's activities. A number of them are very talented writers and artists, and . . ." Mr. Polansky paused for a moment and we could all tell he was about to unload a bombshell. "And I think they should be offered the opportunity to work with us on the *Tarmac*."

"It sounds like a sellout to me," said Rick.

Eddie and Denise both nodded in agreement.

"It's not intended to be," said Mr. Polansky. "It's just something I wanted to bring up for your consideration. At the same time I would like to remind you not to sell your classmates short. It would be easy to lump all of the *Landing Strip* staff members together with Steve, but it wouldn't be fair. Wouldn't you agree, Jessie?"

When a teacher puts you on the spot like that and

136

obviously expects only one response, there's not very much you can do. You have to agree whether you actually do or not. Fortunately, Jessie honestly did agree with him.

"Very much so," she replied. The sincerity in Jessie's voice was unmistakable, and she was so adamant in her conviction that she won over the rest of us instantly. "The people who worked for the *Landing Strip* out of loyalty or friendship with Steve wouldn't come near us with a ten-foot pole anyway. The people who were really interested in writing would probably want to continue and would probably welcome the opportunity to work on the *Tarmac* with open arms. I think we would all benefit from the experience, and I'm all for it."

Mr. Polansky was nodding his head and smiling proudly like a loving grandfather. For a moment I thought he was going to hop over his desk and give Jessie a bear hug. He was very pleased with her, but I could understand exactly how he felt. I was, too.

"And if I may be so bold," said Mr. Renaldo with a wide grin, "I'd like to be the first recruit from the *Landing Strip* to sign up with the *Tarmac*."

It was clear that the two teachers had spoken about this possibility earlier because Mr. Polansky immediately patted Mr. Renaldo on the shoulder to welcome him to the team. The arrangement seemed to go over fine with everyone, and before too long we were laughing and joking and having the victory party we had expected.

It had been a long time coming.

CHAPTER 34

T HERE are a lot of good things about writing a book. It can be a very valuable learning experience, and I recommend it highly to everyone.

As I said at the beginning, this is really Jessie's story — or at least, I intended it to be. I ended up writing a lot more about myself and Rebecca than I had expected to, but I guess I was only kidding myself to think that I could leave her out of what is probably the only book I'll ever write. I've said it time after time, and I'll say it again: Knowing Rebecca was the best thing that ever happened to me. We've reached the point where we can be friends now. But there's still too much feeling there on my part for us ever to be really close friends. Maybe that will change in time. Writing about it has helped me put our relationship in perspective. I know I'll never make the same mistakes again.

I also no longer fear that I'll never meet anyone so right for me.

Jessie tells me that there are a lot of fish in the sea. She's probably right, but I know I'm always going to remember the one that got away.

I guess that's just human nature.